ATAVISTS

ATAVISTS

stories

Lydia Millet

W. W. NORTON & COMPANY

Independent Publishers Since 1923

I'm grateful to my agent, Maria Massie, and to Tom Mayer, Elizabeth Riley, and many others at Norton who have helped with this book, including Don Rifkin, Anna Oler, Steve Colca, Steve Attardo, Nneoma Amadi-obi, and Amy Robbins. I want to thank my friends Sarah Cotten, Zandy Hartig, and Marty Hipsky for their readings of "Therapist," "Cultist," and "Futurist," respectively, and also offer my thanks to Bianca Urbina for her generosity in reviewing "Cosmetologist."

For information about permission to reproduce selections from this book, write to Permissions, W. W. Norton & Company, Inc., 500 Fifth Avenue, New York, NY 10110

For information about special discounts for bulk purchases, please contact W. W. Norton Special Sales at specialsales@wwnorton.com or 800-233-4830

Manufacturing by Lakeside Book Company
Book design by Anna Oler

ISBN 978-1-324-07441-0

W. W. Norton & Company, Inc., 500 Fifth Avenue, New York, NY 10110
www.wwnorton.com

W. W. Norton & Company Ltd., 15 Carlisle Street, London W1D 3BS

1 0 9 8 7 6 5 4 3 2 1

CONTENTS

ATAVISTS

TOURIST

She was courting her own disgust, these days. The way she'd picked at her knee scabs as a kid—knowing it would end in blood but doing it anyway. Revulsion was a stimulant.

The surest route to that stimulation was the feed of a guy who'd once been a friend. Not a close friend but one she'd respected, back then. In recent years he seemed out of reach to the likes of her: neither rich nor well-connected. As so many of his other contacts on social media appeared to be. He was a busy man, a consultant on public-art projects. The work was rewarding, of course, but the real path to redemption, for him, lay in fatherhood.

His tiny daughter was a paragon. He'd relate his dialogues with her in the comments on his Instagram—conversations that showcased her innocence and powers of perception. Along with the wisdom of his sensitive answers.

One dialogue concerned an incident, some centuries before, when a famous man of science had been burned at the stake. Yes! Father and daughter had discussed this dreadful event—they had to. Because the tiny daughter was *always* engaged in the learning process, be it precalculus far beyond her years, the careful study of wildflowers plucked from their own tangled and picturesque garden, or, in this case, the history of the Inquisition.

To comfort her, her father said the person had, by means of his immolation, "dispersed his atoms back into the universe he loved."

The phrase allowed him to illustrate key attributes of himself.

First, that he, like the scientist, knew some physics. For was it not physics that allowed us all to understand how the particles that make up being flow across time, in seeming infinitude, through the bodies of the living and celestial alike? Do we not breathe in the very same particles that traveled through the lungs of Julius Caesar as he died?

Second, it showed he could transmute a tale of violent execution into romantic poetry. For the scientist had perished on a noble altar: the pursuit of knowledge.

And third, it showed how he wished to manifest for his tiny, adorable daughter (and in passing, his several thousand followers) the fineness of his sentiments.

How flawed we are, he acknowledged in another comment. We cast our sins even beyond the planet, now! Into low Earth orbit, for example, where lethal space junk floated in a massive debris field. The outermost garbage dump of a civilization imploding. And none too slowly, either.

But one thing he *could* do was uphold the sacred trust of raising a child. Teaching her that, even upon this sadly devastated sphere, the two of them could bear witness to the wonders that remained.

To attest to that wonder, he posted portraits of the tiny daughter with gentle beams of light falling across her doe-like face. She could be seen in soft focus with a book open across her lap, solemn in her attention. Solving math puzzles on a table in the living room, beneath a soaring vaulted ceiling. Walking in the dappled shade of a suburban bower, a sprig of frail blossoms tucked behind one ear. Or tenderly cradling a beloved doll.

But he did not stop there. His wife was a paragon too. A genius as well as a beauty. He was humbled by her excellence.

Often he referred to her using an honorific: Dr. Pedersen. She was an expert in chaos theory. She'd written a book on the subject and hailed from an enlightened nation in northern Europe where the weather was cold but the government warm. Free health care, for example, was the birthright of its citizens—sixteen months of paid parental leave for single mothers, even!

His wife was blond and lovely and wore cat-eye reading glasses.

Uxorious was the term that came to mind. An antiquated word for men who displayed an unctuous adoration of their spouses.

There were other words for it now.

"He's a wife guy, Mom," said Sam when she showed him the feed. He shrugged. "It's a thing."

The preening was unbearable. Yet Trudy checked the account compulsively, indignant every time. Caught in a cycle of presentation and condemnation like bad reality TV.

Contempt was natural—defensive, probably, and a form of catharsis. But she wasn't uplifted by her daily practice of revulsion. If anything, she was debased by it.

Still, she returned.

Sometimes she thought she was waiting for him to step forward with a confession.

The scales have fallen from my eyes, he might suddenly admit. I see it clearly now. The coy obscenity of how I praise others. Only to elevate myself.

———————

She'd tried to get away for a while. Signed out of her accounts, not viewed the pictorial curations, not read the snarky tweets.

Used her phone only to speak. As her parents and grandparents had before her.

It hadn't lasted. She had to go back. In the barely three weeks she was absent from social, two posts escaped her notice: a veiled reference to a traumatic miscarriage and a regretful announcement of a marital separation.

She was missing the performance of other lives. And thus the gap between that performance and the lives themselves.

Because when she went out in real life there was often a reframing of the images, as they related to actual events. She'd seen shots of Amy, her old college roommate, caught up in the rapture of a weekend jet-ski adventure. Along with her attractive husband and children.

The family knew how to enjoy themselves, was the message. And look good doing it.

Whereas Trudy herself, by contrast, had just posted a video of a stray dog hungrily licking at a used diaper. In someone's spilled garbage at the curb. Why not? It made her wince. And also laugh.

After she laughed, she'd taken the dog a bowl of scraps. No one should have to eat from diapers.

But then, at a coffee shop in Los Feliz, the scoop was that Amy's husband Buzz, a marathon runner, had plantar fasciitis he hadn't bothered to seek treatment for, because men, doctors, you know, what*ever*. He'd started a special, extra-rugged marathon in the Sierras—they'd all driven up to represent and splashed out for a nice hotel—but then had to stop at mile three. Because of foot pain.

There they were, feeling let down in the hotel room, so Amy had booked the jet-skiing as a consolation prize.

And their daughter Liza, who'd looked like a swimsuit model on her jet ski, had secretly gotten married to a twenty-year-old DACA kid. Though she was eighteen and still in high school. She'd shown up for dinner late one night, plunked down her backpack at the door, and announced she was married. Had the certificate to prove it.

Which was awesome in a *way*, right? Amy and Buzz were supportive, not that the DACA thing was the *reason*—if he hadn't been a Dreamer they might have accepted the marriage too. Dysfunctional, sure, but also a lingering aftereffect of the pandemic, probably. COVID had left teenagers with no sense of normalcy, desperate to form lasting social attachments.

That was what Amy's therapist said, anyway.

Luckily the boy-husband was smart, hardworking, and motivated as hell, but he did have an internet porn addiction. It wasn't a huge deal: he'd agreed to seek help.

He was a great kid. And handsome!

However, Liza was going off to college at the end of summer, so they'd have to pay for an apartment for the two of them off-campus. He was living with them now, to cut costs and help shorten his commute, which was how Buzz found out about the internet porn.

They hadn't told their daughter. Instead, Buzz had taken his son-in-law aside. It was between the two of them, he'd said. As men.

Although he told Amy, of course.

"Personally," she told Amy, "I'd rather have seen a mention of that than a picture of jet-skiing."

"Yeah, but Trudy. *You* posted a video of a dog eating shit."

"Also, how are his personal sex habits Buzz's business? It's just porn."

"The thing is, it was fetish porn."

"Really? What fetish?"

"Can't go there, Trudy. I seriously can't."

"Well. *That* was a tease."

The posters wanted to be known. A true, authentic yearning. The first steps were being seen. And heard.

They had the first steps down, but then they stopped. Got stuck on the approach. The alternate selves they put on public view, their humblebrags or glamour shots, were like the stick figures kindergartners drew. In a foreground with no perspective, where faces, apples, and the moon were the exact same size.

Another guy she followed was a trendy futurist in her department. An arrogant technocrat. He'd given a widely shared TED talk from a paper that had never been peer reviewed—empty bombast full of vague distortions.

Based on the popularity of that talk, which passed for mainstream relevance in academia, he'd received a generous salary hike. Despite his lack of tenure.

She should probably read him anyway.

His posts dispensed with punctuation. Even the use of a period marked you as geriatric, in social media and texts. As a millennial he strove to bridge the divide between himself and Gen Z. Saw himself as a postmodern Ayn Rand, minus the senseless logical contradictions. Empowerment of the ego was his deal. He'd give the eboys a purpose, dammit. Beyond the hair selfies.

When a fresh subculture grew up, you wanted it to have an

edge. Like the punks or hippies. But the young subcultures on social seemed to be void of ideology. Beyond naming and shaming each other for perceived identity bias. If they had an ideology, it contained no ideas.

Pure narcissism. The point was not to be but to seem. Prettier, cooler, righter.

Competition was the driver. They couldn't see how they were echoing the models of market capital. In a frenzy of having to seem better than.

And let the gesture stand in for a soul.

Sam was fourteen and got most of his input from gaming circles and YouTube monologues on pop culture and trends. Some of which, she had to admit, were more intriguing than the information he was receiving at school.

She didn't blame him.

He was an affectionate boy, for his age. Occasionally he still took her hand. Of his own accord. Held it, even, for a minute or two.

Not in public, of course.

But he was saddened by her ignorance.

Of language. Of the world. The infinite landscape of the internet.

Once she'd asked him what BTS was, after he made a passing reference, and he'd stared at her with his mouth hanging open. Slack-jawed.

You never heard of *BTS*? he asked.

Not that he was a fan, he assured her. K-pop was of no interest to him. He preferred the dead godheads. Say, Bowie or Cobain.

His point was that major phenomena went right over her head.

As though the aurora borealis was rippling across the sky in glorious hues and she was bent over tying her shoelace. Forever.

She'd vowed, in her youth, never to let herself get old.

In years, of course, she'd age. In skin and bones, movement and muscles. But what she'd believed and insisted, long ago, was that she wouldn't allow herself to *calcify*. Wouldn't become, as her own parents had, irrelevance in human form. Enacting automatic functions they'd performed for decades, bound by routine. And never to diverge from it.

As the futurist colleague might say, or a comedian she'd heard— in the context of old, white racists—failing to update their OS.

But then, here she was. Living in the minor corner of the real. In a forgotten country.

Without TikTok edits or multiplayer games. Barely even a meme.

It didn't help to watch the same videos Sam watched or hang out in the background, making his bed or picking up dirty, turtled socks from his floor as he gamed. Listening as his friends, on speaker, issued torrents of delighted or combative words.

Whose meanings she simply could not decode.

In the new world she would always be a tourist.

Here and there she found an account she admired. Elements of autobiography might be present in the background, but there was an openness, too. A turning outward to the world.

She knew relief, scrolling through those feeds. A relief that felt like affection—the surprising luck of finding good company.

The images suggested their authors had a sense of scale. That it was possible for the photo boxes to be windows instead of mirrors.

One of the best belonged to a woman she'd met at a mutual friend's party. She lived just a few blocks away, as it turned out, and after the party the two of them had sometimes run into each other at a corner mini-mart they could both walk to.

The feed was subtle and self-effacing—animals, plants, and signage the woman spotted as she walked her beloved dog around their neighborhood. Her photos were understated and forlorn, and when she commented the words were subtle and self-effacing too. Trudy followed it for some time.

Then the woman died of cancer, though she was only in her forties. Trudy heard about it from the mutual friend. And scrolled through the feed again.

The final post was a video of the woman dancing. Alone with her dog in her apartment, when she must have already been sick, to a sad old song. As the dog followed her small, graceful movements with faithful, patient head-turnings.

Watching it, Trudy got tears in her eyes.

But then a cousin who lived across the country, and perhaps had never quite understood the nuances of her relative's personality, came to the city to help clean out the apartment.

She posted her journey of discovery on the decedent's account.

A lesson, Trudy thought, not to leave your phone lying around with the apps signed in to.

To guard your passwords well.

And not to be trusting and open while you died.

The journey included items found at the bottom of the decedent's purse: receipts from restaurants, ticket stubs, and a couple of fortune-cookie fortunes.

But one scrap of paper in particular spoke volumes to the cousin. It bore a piece of text ascribed—mistakenly—to Wordsworth.

Googling, Trudy saw the text had been penned by an unknown writer at a greeting-card company.

And she realized: it had to be from a guy who begged outside the mini-mart. She'd put money on it, if anyone offered her a bet.

He'd been stationed there for many months, with his orange tabby cat and a series of grimy, striped Mexican blankets. If you gave him a buck or two, he'd hand you a piece of writing in return. A Bible verse, a pamphlet, or sometimes a cookie fortune from the Chinese takeout place next door. You shoved it into your bag, not wanting to throw it away right in front of him, and then forgot it was there.

But the cousin decided the text on the paper scrap represented the decedent's overall philosophy.

She made a large, flowery graphic and put it up *In Memoriam*: the very last post on the feed. Accompanied by the comment, These were the words she lived by.

"Happiness is being loved by pets and children. Running in the grass with no shoes on. And walking in the rain with no umbrella."   *—William Wordsworth*

Superseding all that came before: the capstone on a life.

Deepfakes were a concern to Sam. Along with AI, which was doing a friend's English homework and earning him a B+.

Digital effigies of leaders and celebrities, he said, would soon be so abundant that the fictional would be inseparable from the real.

"Isn't it already?" asked Trudy.

This conversation took place while she was fixing him dinner. He enjoyed the meals she prepared from boxes and jars.

One night a week he went to stay with his father, per the custody arrangement, who unlike her was a cook—made soufflés and sautéed semi-obscure vegetables. Broccoli rabe. Japanese eggplant. Mustard greens. Spices and sauces were involved.

She used to find those dishes tasty, back when they were married, but Sam preferred to eat one simple meal repeatedly. Plus the carrot sticks and bell peppers she shoehorned in on the side as the price he had to pay for mac-and-cheeses and frozen mini-pizzas.

She understood. The first time she'd had her own apartment, after college, she'd eaten fruit pies for supper many days in a row.

Frozen. Then thawed. With dollops of Cool Whip on top.

No one can stop me! she'd thought.

A small bud of triumph had unfurled its petals. Resplendent.

And that had proved to be accurate. No one had lifted a finger.

Now influencers lectured her on how to become her best self. That self might be realized through leafy greens and quinoa, plus other "ancient grains." And no gluten, probably.

She slid the mini-pizzas into the oven.

"It'll be way worse," said Sam. "*Worse* than it is now."

"I worry more about everything we absorb without realizing we're even doing it," she said. "The way misinformation colonizes us."

"Not only misinformation," agreed Sam. "Even other people's feelings. Being mad. Or afraid. It's kind of like, catching."

Her generation didn't like their consumer data being collected. But she wasn't convinced it was the manipulations of companies and interest groups that alarmed them—more the sneaking suspicion that, one of these days, Jeff Bezos might decide to interest himself in their vibrator-buying habits.

"Maybe what's worse than things being taken from us," she said to Sam, "are the things being given to us. The things that permeate us. And silently change our minds. Without us noticing."

The new world was a vast frontier, she thought. Into which we all set sail with a supreme confidence. As wide and deep as the ocean.

And an ignorance still wider and deeper.

Ignorance of the past. Casual indifference to the future.

He had friends from school and the skatepark that he'd made the old-fashioned way, through the location of his body in space.

But also many friends he'd never seen in the flesh. Who lived in far-flung places. Some of them six or seven time zones away. He'd met them playing Minecraft.

"Met" had a different meaning, for him.

Some parents frowned on those virtual friendships. The supposed friends might be sexual predators. Kidnappers or identity thieves.

Sam scoffed at those suggestions. His friends didn't know his street address. Or last name.

"I'm not going to be *abducted*, Mom."

"So none of them can spy on you? No one can trace you by your IP address, or whatever?"

He rolled his eyes.

"The Minecraft community doesn't have a lot of haters. And I'm not an *idiot*, Mom. Anyway, there are lots of bad guys IRL. And *they* could be standing right next to me."

"How reassuring."

He patted her on the shoulder.

The love she felt for him was so piercing she almost wished it away. Not the love itself, only its urgent quality. She might blunt *that*, if she could. To make it easier to bear. Even the knowledge that in four years he'd be leaving, because it was what they did when the clock struck eighteen, was like a pocketful of stones.

Trying to fall asleep, now and then, she remembered a magazine writer who, some time ago, had posted a blog entry on how she felt she could recover from one of her children's deaths. If such a death occurred. But not from the death of her husband.

She'd asked whether this made her a bad mother and defiantly answered her own question: no. But for many readers, the answer had been yes. Some feminists had supported the writer; others had pilloried her. It was reprehensible, those others said. How would her children feel? When they grew up and read her words?

The father was a writer too. Well-known. So the blog entry also served as an endorsement.

Reading it, what Trudy had thought was: Jesus, lady. You're tempting fate. By invoking the possible death of your children.

She thought, And you may well be deluded about whose death would end up hitting you the hardest. How can you know? You can't.

You may just be a fabricator, stirring up publicity. But if you're not deluded or a liar, one thing you are for sure, in your superficial glibness, is goddamn fucking lucky.

Never to have lost a child.

She saw Amy again for a mani-pedi. Didn't often indulge, herself, but Amy said she knew a cheap place with strong Russian ladies who put real muscle into their callus work.

Afterward they'd get lunch.

"Hey," Trudy asked her as they sat in side-by-side chairs having the balls of their feet rasped, "do you ever look at Justin's Instagram?"

Amy knew the art consultant too. The two of them had met him three years after graduation, when they decided impulsively to attend an alumni function on campus. Never attended one again, but that night they'd met him and gotten sloppy drunk. Left the fundraiser and wandered down frat row ringing doorbells, outlandishly claiming to be EMTs. Looking for a case of alcohol poisoning someone had called in.

It had been Hell Week.

"Oh my God! *Yes!*" said Amy. "That doll thing?"

"What doll thing?"

"He had to take it down!"

"Wait. Back up, please."

"So you know, his daughter—"

"I think we *all* know his daughter."

"So he put up this photo of her holding a baby doll, right?"

"I remember it."

"But the doll was African American!"

"Oh yeah? I didn't notice. The filter, maybe."

"And they're as white as milk! His wife is *Scandinavian*. Practically a blond goddess. Like, Aryan."

"Technically the Aryans could have brown hair, too. Like Hitler."

"So you can't *do* that, right? Obviously."

"A white kid can't have a black doll?"

"And post it on social? Are you kidding? White ownership of the black body? Trudy. He literally lost, like, a thousand followers."

She should have felt smug at his dethroning. It was the flex too far.

But here she was, watching a manicurist kneel at her feet. And slough off dead skin.

They weren't Russian, by the way, she mentioned to Amy as they left. Yellow sunflower posters with a blue background. Ukrainian. For sure.

When she picked Sam up after a night at his dad's he was typically depressed. Not always—he could be cheerful and invigorated if they'd done something together—but usually.

Once, on a Saturday afternoon, he was more mournful than usual. He sat in the backseat, which he preferred when he wasn't in the mood to talk, listening to music.

It made her feel like a chauffeur.

"So what did you and your dad get up to?" she asked.

Grudgingly he removed one earbud.

"Pardon?"

"So what did you guys do?"

"Nothing. He was on his phone."

"Oh," she said, and felt the familiar pang of hurt. On his behalf. "I'm sorry to hear that. He gets caught up in his work, doesn't he."

"I guess."

"He does," she said. "Even on weekends."

He hesitated. She thought he was getting ready to put the earbud back in, but instead he said quietly, "He's just not that interested in me, Mom. I could be anyone."

"Oh, that's not true!"

"It is. He doesn't even know me."

She was torn. Always confused over how much she should say about his father.

They were passing a park.

"*I* know what we'll do," she said, and turned into the parking lot.

"*What*," said Sam, sullen.

"Let's get out," she said. "Leave your earbuds. This'll be quick."

She stepped out as he lagged. Resistant. Finally stood and shut the car door.

A grassy hill stretched in front of them.

"Now run," she said.

"What? I don't *want* to, Mom."

"Just run!" she said.

She started.

"Come on!" she yelled back at him. "We have to run!"

"Why?"

"Because they're chasing us!"

"Who?"

"All of them! Everyone!"

"Everyone *who*?"

"Just run!"

He picked up his feet slightly. Still resisting. She went backward a bit, beckoning. He sped up.

Half smiling, then.

He was in the race.

"Run! Run for your life!"

As they crested the hill, he pulled ahead of her. Faster and faster. Sprinting hard. He was thin and lithe.

She wouldn't give up, she thought.

He would always be ahead of her.

But she could see him. For now.

She tore after, breathing heavily. Had to slow down, but she could follow. Across the baseball diamond. Over the yellow grass between the trees. Past the slide and the swings and the jungle gym.

Past the whole playground. Into the far distance.

DRAMATIST

Her brother was twenty-two, back living at home after college and working at some big-box store. On his days off, he LARPed. Medieval Fantasy was his chosen theme.

And yeah, she judged him for it. Because he didn't post about it on social, but his girlfriend did. He'd met her at an event in the Inland Empire and it turned out she lived nearby. In the Valley.

In the posts the two of them would have streaks of blood on their faces, in supposedly artful patterns, and be wearing necklaces made of squirrel or rat skulls.

"Gross," Liza had said.

"They're just resin," said Nick.

In the pictures and videos they'd be brandishing axes. Which he called halberds. Or swords. Carrying shields painted with dragons or crosses. Standing around with other losers, similarly outfitted.

Chaya favored leather bodices with buckles in front. She made Nick wear matching vests.

Then she'd tag Liza. And Liza's friends would see it.

"Your brother used to be so cool," they'd say, shaking their heads. "*Everyone* thought he was cool. What *happened* to him?"

It blew past cringe. Straight to humiliating.

He didn't bother to check the posts—barely looked at social. So he didn't perceive his own humiliation. Or hers.

She tried to make him see by using words like "loser."

He said she didn't have to like it. It was *his* deal.

"Not when Chaya's putting it *out* there. It makes you look like a loser. And by association, me."

"Listen, Liza," he said. "Is *history* for losers?"

"Extremely. It's like, a million details of how we trashed the world and killed off the people who didn't have as many guns. Then tried to pass it off as the best idea ever. Which maybe you already know, as a Stanford graduate? Anyway, this isn't history. It's Medieval Fantasy."

"What I meant was, is it *loserish* to be, say, a Civil War re-enactor?"

"Are you kidding me? Yes! Do you see titans of industry spending their downtime on Civil War re-enactments? Rock stars or AOC? No. Who you see is losers. And white supremacists. Big overlap."

"So in your book, if a person's not a titan of industry or a rock star, they're a loser."

She shrugged. "If the shoe fits . . ."

"So to you, like, 99.99 percent of the population are losers."

"I'd say if you have a degree that cost your family three hundred grand but you're working at Cost Plus carrying jumbo bags of shrimp into freezers and spending your Saturdays acting out fake battles with Nerf swords, the odds are pretty good."

"It's not Cost Plus. They don't have freezers at Cost Plus. Don't you even know where I work? And the weapons aren't *Nerf.* Jesus."

He was writing a fantasy script when he wasn't at work or dressing up as the Son of Ragnar. Claimed the RPGs facilitated his "creative process."

A pilot, he said, for an ongoing series. On a streaming platform. His goal was to be a writer-producer.

Once, while Luis was away visiting cousins in Escondido, she saw part of the script on her brother's laptop.

Which she was not supposed to look at.

EXT. CELTIC FORTRESS—TWILIGHT
Dryads and nymphs cavort among the waving trees. Scantily clad.

Then blank. She scrolled up. Nothing—it was the first page.

That night at dinner she said "scantily clad" twice. Slipped it into the conversation.

Nick didn't notice.

So then she mentioned dryads and nymphs. She'd googled them. Weren't dryads the spirits of trees? she asked. If so, how did they differ from nymphs? And wait—where did the naiads come in?

He went on eating his spaghetti. Apparently thought it was normal to be talking about dryads and nymphs.

Or he was zoned out. As usual.

"So did the ancient Celts build *fortresses?*" she asked her father. "Or more like, just hide out in the hills and rocks?"

Out of the blue: her dad had been talking about Ironmans. And wasn't known for his expertise on ancient Celts.

Nick put down his fork. It clattered on the plate.

"Have you been reading my *screenplay?*"

"On accident. It didn't take long. I spotted both two lines of it. As I walked past."

"Liza, you shouldn't have done that," said their mother. "But also, you must have been looking at another document. He's been working on it for *months.* Right, Nicky?"

"It's the beginning of the current *iteration,*" said Nick. "There are others."

"Can I read those ones, too?" asked Liza. "I could give you notes. Any reader is better than none. They say."

"When hell freezes over?"

"The deal was, though," said their dad, chewing and swallowing, "that you produce a script in six months. Free room and board. A day job for gas and spending money. Then you find an agent to shop it. Six months more. So . . . how long has it been?"

"I can't believe this! *She* violates my personal, intellectual space. And *I'm* being waterboarded?"

"She was wrong to do so," said their dad, "but we still need to have the conversation. Deliverables, Nick."

"He's been back in the house for fourteen months," said Liza. Just trying to be helpful.

"We weren't measuring from *graduation,*" said Nick. "We were measuring from September. I had the summer as a grace period."

"Sorry. Eleven months. So you already have an agent, right?"

"I sent out queries. I've had some interest."

"Liza, you may be excused," said their mother. "Go ahead and start loading up the dishwasher."

"Show business is *really* hard," said her brother as she picked up her plate.

"Famously," said their dad. "What's not so hard, maybe, with an honors degree from Stanford, is moving on from the big-box store."

Loading the dishwasher, she felt light and free.

Hummed "This Is My Fight Song."

Then headed back to the dining room to collect more plates.

"It's asymmetrical," Nick was saying. "Liza elopes, when she's a high-school *senior*, with an undocumented rando—"

"He's a *Dreamer*!" she burst out. "He's lived here all his life!"

"—that she met at a convenience store—"

"A deli!"

"—and you roll out the red carpet! And here *I* am, just trying to make—"

"I can't believe he's weaponizing my marriage," said Liza.

"Liza!" said their mom. "You've already been excused. You can clear the table later."

"What are you gonna do next? Smile proudly and clap your hands when she pumps out Guatemalan babies?"

"Oh my *God*!" said Liza. "You orange-faced *fascist*!"

"If the shoe fits . . ."

"They use birth control," said her mother.

"Mom! That's *completely private*!" said Liza.

"OK," said her father, raising his hands. "This is officially too much for me to deal with. At the dinner table. Nicholas, you need to check your privilege. Big-time. And Liza, stop baiting him."

If Luis had been there, Nick would never have said that. When he was around Nick tried to impress him. Rope him into the LARPing, even. Luis always smiled and shook his head. Too busy working for minimum wage while studying for the bar. He was taking an online course.

Fine, then. The gloves were off.

He came to her room before he went to bed and apologized.

"I was acting out," he said. "You *know* me. I don't think like that. It's stupid garbage. Luis is awesome. Obviously. But even if he wasn't, I wouldn't pin the blame on his ethnicity. In that moment, I took the racism and ran with it. It was almost like Tourette's. Like, I wanted the worst possible thing to come out of my mouth."

"That's not Tourette's. Plus you don't *have* Tourette's. So. Don't be ableist."

"But like, a compulsion. To be hateful."

"Mission accomplished."

"I know. There's no excuse."

Apologies were better than nothing. But she wasn't going to let him off the hook.

Her working theory was that there wasn't, in fact, another "iteration" of the script. Or if there was, it sucked.

Chaya was the weak link. Chaya would know. Not whether the script was bad—she, possibly, didn't have the critical chops for that—but whether it existed.

And *she* would have a friendly conversation. Unlike Nick.

So the next time Chaya was over—while Luis was at work and Nick was downstairs—Liza found her in the upstairs bathroom. The door stood open as she stripped off her LARPing kit. On the counter beside the sink some kind of white fur was lumped like a dead animal.

"What's that?" asked Liza.

"Viking fur mantle. Arctic fox. But faux, obviously."

"Fur is murder," nodded Liza.

"Totally."

"So how'd the event go today?" she asked.

Sometimes they did fighter practice in a local park. Small-scale. Other times they made a pilgrimage to a massive event. They'd drive for hours to attend.

"Nick got bored. He wants to try Dystopia Rising. For a change, he said. But we don't have kits, so we'd have to start from scratch. And I have *zero* interest in dystopic. Cannibal Mutants? Please. Everyone's hideous."

She started to take off her wig. Long and burgundy. A comb got stuck in her own hair.

"Do you need help?"

"Thanks. I got it."

She set it down atop the fake fur shawl. The wig had leaf litter in it. And what looked like a dead spider.

"Yeah, no," said Liza. "Cannibal Mutants don't sound great."

Chaya leaned into the mirror to wipe off a facial tattoo.

"Depressing," she said. "I'm not into post-apocalyptic."

"I wouldn't be either. It's like, seriously, guys. The apocalypse is *not* gonna be that fun."

"I'd rather try Vampire. I could be up for Vampire. You go to vampire courts in different cities. Though there aren't as many events being held. Since the stupid pandemic."

"Listen, though," said Liza. "I had this idea. You know how Nick is so secretive? About that show pilot he's been writing?"

Chaya turned and looked at her. Rolled her eyes. "Do I *ever*," she said. Then faced the mirror again to take off her huge ear-rings. They were fake bone spirals, supposed to look like gauges.

Her father wouldn't let her stretch out her earlobes with giant holes, she'd told Liza. You'll look like a woman in *National Geographic*, he had said.

Clearly, racist.

"So I know this woman," Liza pressed. "An agent's assistant. In Century City. I figure, if I could get her a copy of the script? She might be able to *do* something for him."

Not a lie, in fact. She *did* know an agent's assistant. The older sister of her best friend since kindergarten.

"Oh, wow. Did you tell him?"

"I can't. He's afraid to take that next step. And you know what? I think it's fear of success."

"That might be true!" said Chaya. "Fear of success!"

"It would explain a lot," said Liza. "My parents say what's holding him back, with the pilot script, is a fear of failure. But what if it's fear of *success*? We might never know!"

"So what's your idea?"

"Maybe you can get the script for me. And I could send it to her."

"Like, get it secretly?"

"He might thank you later."

"Oh, man. I don't know . . . and it might not be finished yet. He won't tell me."

"But even if it's not. What if she *saw* something in him? Right?"

"I guess . . ."

"Think about it. That's all I'm asking."

"Think about what, Liza?"

Nick, at the top of the stairs. Wearing his very own Viking mantle. Brown, not white. Baggy brown leggings with straps. Also, a pointed skull dangling over his chest.

Bigger than the ones previously spotted on Instagram.

"What's *that* skull of?" asked Liza. Trying for a redirect.

"Possum. Think about what?"

"Is it resin?"

"No, it's a real possum," said Chaya. "I bought it for him on our half-year anniversary."

"Doesn't it have germs?"

"They, like, boil the shit out of them," said Chaya.

"Answer my question," said Nick.

"Just if she feels like hanging out tonight and ordering pizza. We could watch *Ferris*."

"No one wants to watch *Ferris*, Liza. Everyone saw *Ferris* in high school."

"Or it could be a new release," Liza suggested.

"Anyway, we're busy," said Nick.

OK, she hadn't *really* asked if Chaya wanted to hang out, but it still stung a bit.

He always said he was busy.

Movie night wasn't a bad idea, though. She invited Selma and Katie, who happened to be her two friends most horrified by Nick's current personal iteration.

Selma, honestly, could be straight-up mean. She'd been super bitchy when Liza eloped with Luis. Whispering to their other friends that Liza must be pregnant and would be like one of those fat girls who suddenly gave birth in a stall in the school bathroom.

Which didn't make any sense, as an insult. If you got married because you were knocked up, you wouldn't have the baby in a toilet stall.

She'd written Teen Mom on Liza's locker in lipstick. Liza'd known it was her because she'd lent her that lipstick. MAC Odyssey.

They only started speaking again after Selma met Luis at a party and decided he was hot. Then she apologized, saying she totally would have had his baby herself, and offered to buy Liza a new tube of Odyssey.

Except by then the shade was discontinued. She still owed Liza a lipstick. But Liza had forgiven her because she'd heard from Katie that Selma's stepdad was a serious creep. He'd taken her shopping, for example, saying he was buying a bikini for her mother as a surprise gift, and made Selma model them in a changing room.

"Which," said Katie, "just *no*, right? First off, who gets a bikini as a gift? You buy your own bikinis. Selma said he made her try on like ten of them. Don't tell her I told you."

Katie wasn't mean by herself but was a Selma follower. A threat multiplier of Selma.

They cued up *Clueless*, even though they'd seen it several times, because they could all agree about nineties stuff, and did face masks as they waited for the pizza delivery guy. Liza's parents were going out on a date night, her mother wearing an unfortunate purple dress that Selma spotted as they tried to slip quietly out the front door.

Her mom was afraid of Selma.

And rightly so.

"I heart that dress, Mrs. B!" said Selma sweetly. But then the door clicked shut and she turned to Liza. "She needs to invest in some Spanx. Like, yesterday."

"You're body-shaming my *mother*?" asked Liza.

"It's not shaming. It's helping to maximize her potential."

Nick came down when they were watching the movie. With the pizza box open on the coffee table.

He loitered at the end of the couch, staring at Alicia Silverstone.

"Hey, Nick," said Katie. "Help yourself. We got a large."

"Nick's too busy for pizza tonight," said Liza.

"Oh yeah?" said Selma. "What are you busy with, Nick? Up there alone in your bedroom?"

"Working," he said, and reached down for a slice.

"I thought you worked at Costco," said Katie.

"He's writing a screenplay," said Liza.

"Oh yeah?" asked Selma. "Does it have Ragnarok in it?"

"Ragnarok?" asked Katie.

"You know, his cosplay name," said Selma.

"It's not Ragnarok, Selma," said Nick, taking a bite. "Ragnarok is the end of the world. In Norse mythology. The world is consumed by flames. And I don't do cosplay. It's live-action role-playing."

"I thought role-playing was, like, a sex deal," said Selma. "Like, S&M."

"Uh, no," said Nick.

"I mean, it *is*," said Selma. A thin string of cheese dangled from her slice, and she lifted up the slice to catch the cheese on her tongue. "But it's not what *you* do, I guess. It'd be hard with all those mouse skulls getting in the way. If someone tried to do sadistic things to me wearing a mouse skull necklace, I'd laugh my ass off."

"There's no S&M in Medieval Fantasy. At least, not the events we go to. Sorry to disappoint you."

"Your girlfriend's kind of hot, though. What's-her-name. Kaia."

"Chaya."

"Does she wear push-up bras under those leather bustiers?"

"You'd have to ask her."

"The women can pull it off, because for them it's a basic whore vibe, right? But with the guys, it's like, Lose the helmet, buddy. And the leggings look like footie pajamas. That toddlers wear."

"The guys should just wear normal pants," agreed Katie.

"Luckily we're not trying to titillate little high-school girls," said Nick.

"Burn!" said Selma. "But it makes sense. It's all dumpy old nerds, at those things, right?"

"If you define *old* as above drinking age, sure," said Nick. "There are about fifty million participants, internationally. And yeah, the games took a hit in COVID. But they're coming back."

"So what's the screenplay about? Does it have Vikings in it?"

"That's my cue," said Nick. He bent over, took a second slice, and turned to go.

"Your brother is *so* tragic, Liza," said Selma, while he was going up the stairs and could obviously hear. "He's a cautionary tale."

Their mother still tidied his room for him—he gave her permission by leaving it trashed. Whereas Liza and Luis's room was clean as a whistle. So her mother never went in.

And after she picked up his room, she washed his clothes for him. Though that didn't always work out. Once she'd put a wool costume thing in the dryer and it shrank down to baby size.

"Mom, that doublet cost a hundred dollars," Nick had whined.

While Liza and Luis, like grownups, did their own laundry.

OK, it was mostly Luis. He folded shirts so neatly they looked like they were on display in a Gap.

But the upside was, maybe *their mother* could be the vector. If Liza could find a printout in a drawer or something, then—after reading it, of course—she could place it in a prominent location in the room. Their mother would be drawn to it. Unable to help herself.

So she launched a search while he was at the store. Had a moment of excitement, finding a couple of pages that had fallen down between the bed and the wall, but they turned out to be printouts from a fan website. Of *Outlander*. Had to be Chaya's. *Outlander* was soft porn for middle-aged women, Nick had said.

Then, too, she found a sheaf of papers on his bookshelf, between *The Hobbit* and *The Silmarillion*, but they were from his thesis comparing world-building in Tolkien to world-building in G.R.R.M.

She was sitting on the bed staring at a pile of snack crumbs on the sheet, feeling defeated, when a page corner caught her eye. Sticking out from under the box of a board game.

She crossed the room and grabbed it.

Other papers beneath.

EXT. CELTIC FORTRESS—DUSK

Jackpot.

She sat down on the bed again, the sheaf of paper in her hands. Had a giddy feeling at the unexpected triumph.

> *Dryads and nymphs cavort among the waving trees. Scantily clad.*
> *One dryad begins to sing. A haunting, eerie music.*
> *A cloud crosses the moon.*
> *As she sings, the woodland creatures slowly emerge.*
> *They gather on the lawn. Listening.*
> *Deer, elk, and bears. Badgers, raccoons, and stoats.*

What the hell was a stoat?

A rabbit with her babies. Squirrels. Chipmunks.
We see an owl alight on a branch. Then another. Hawks.
Doves. The birds watch from above, the mammals from
below.
Captured by the music, the animals watch faithfully, their
eyes round and black.
As the dryad dances, casting her mystical spell.

She pictured the woodland creatures hanging out together. Through the miracle of CGI.

So cheesy the audience would laugh.

The more she read, the more her stomach sank.

When she finished, she let the pages rest on her knees and sat there, slumped. Not wanting to move.

Because yeah. The script wasn't even a script. And whatever it was, it was bad.

Even *she* knew that. And she wasn't anyone.

But she didn't feel glad.

She looked around at his books and posters. All the stuff other people had made. Gathered together in his nest. Admired so much. Wanted to imitate.

Like he was a part of it.

But he *wasn't* a part of it. And he would never be.

Except right here. Under the posters and books, in the bedroom he'd slept in since he was three.

She'd wanted to have something *on* him. But now she didn't want to in the least. She wished the script had been perfect. A Celtic fortress for the ages. Or a Saxon fortress. Built to fend off Vikings.

Any fortress at all.

Instead it was a pile of pebbles in the sand. The smooth river rocks they'd thrown across a creek when they were little.

Skip, skip, skip, skip, skip.

The rocks had sunk, covered by water. Gone.

In real life, a hawk would swoop down from its perch and grab one of those baby rabbits. An owl would grab a chipmunk, maybe.

Done and done. Dryad party over.

Sitting on his messy bed, she felt like crying.

What would they *do* to him? The rest of everyone? In their offices and fancy cars, with their buildings and companies?

He was nothing to them.

He used to be a gilded boy. A shining brother. In the swing of the world. Went off to college. Fanfare. He made the honor roll.

Then suddenly he was back here. In his nest.

Beaten before he started.

Why?

An invisible hand was pressing down on him. Maybe a talon. The talon of a CGI hawk, piercing his baby rabbit skin.

She hadn't understood. She'd wanted to yell at him. So she'd picked and picked with her beak.

Now all the resentment lifted off. And left sadness.

Sadness that came in waves, the way sound did.

Or streamed through you like electricity.

Which it was. Along with the rest of the emotions. Just electrical impulses that made you who you were.

The sadness of wanting. The sadness of hope.

FETISHIST

When he first saw the page, his reflex was to laugh. Seemed like a joke. Not the fact that the kid looked at a bit of porn—that was par for the course—but the content. So out of *keeping* with the boy. Who was, in many ways, the son he'd always wanted.

I mean yeah, he said to himself, he already *had* a son, and you probably couldn't love a son more than he loved *his* son.

Though personally, he saw it as a plateau. How much you loved your kids. The love was so much, right out of the gate, that it could never go higher. You were already at the top.

Sure, there were times when you *liked* them less. As people. And more again, over the months and years. That wasn't a plateau. That was like interval training. Sprint, rest. Sprint, rest.

But his son-in-*law*—Luis was a gem. He admired the kid more the longer he knew him. Fair-minded and gentle. He'd do his thankless labor all day, get home, and cook a delicious dinner for the whole family. Afterward he'd clean the kitchen, thank you very much, and then wipe down the table with an eco-friendly surface cleaner.

And he was handy. Hell, he'd go ahead and change the oil in Buzz's SUV. Because, he said, they didn't need to pay out for the labor. He had a cousin who handled the oil disposal, on the up-and-up, at the Jiffy Lube where he worked. Charged the family five bucks.

Then Luis would stay awake studying till three in the morning. Rise at six and head off to his job again.

Buzz knew he studied hard because they shared the common desktop in the rec room.

It had been Buzz's, way back when, but he also had a lap-top from work, so the old home desktop had turned commu-nal. Luis didn't own a PC. And didn't want to use Liza's. He respected her privacy.

After he studied there'd be a long list of legal cases in the browser history. Buzz didn't like to leave tabs open: the bookmark gimmick annoyed him. So he'd gotten into the habit of resorting to the browser history to get back to the sites he needed.

Which was how, it seemed, he'd found a minor catch, in terms of Luis. A porn site—just one page—nestled between legal citations.

He had no beef with porn. It was a product. You jerked off to it. When your wife was too tired. Or as a freebie, for the hell of it. It was a tool. Like any other.

But the porn site Luis had visited had a theme: older women.

It went beyond MILFs. Grandmothers, basically.

Amy had read a self-help book that said contentious subjects between couples were best approached in bed, when men were at their most receptive. Ideally after sex, but also bed in general. He noticed her embracing this technique and had to admit it was effective. Even after she'd told him about it.

Reminded him of an article he'd read on the placebo effect. It said placebos worked, statistically, even if doctors informed their patients they were nothing but sugar pills.

He figured, what was good for the gander was probably OK for the goose, too.

So when he joined her in bed, he told her what he'd seen.

Turned out to be a major tactical error.

"You're saying Luis is into *old ladies*? *Luis*?"

"I mean, they're not bedridden. More . . . you know, seasoned. And kind of comforting."

"Is it real? Or are they just wearing old-lady makeup?"

More likely, he suggested, they were just elderly.

"Maybe it's that Madonna-whore complex," she suggested. "You know—they talk about it. With the Catholic boys. And men."

"He's not really Catholic," said Buzz.

"He grew *up* Catholic. He goes to mass with María Inés."

"That's just to keep her company. She knows he's not a believer."

"Believing's not the point. When it comes to Madonnas and whores. It's the culture."

"I don't see it. There's not really a whore thing, with him. More just the Madonnas, maybe."

"Come on! By definition, the sex workers in the videos take care of the whore part."

"Huh. Well, I guess."

"Oh. Wait. Oh no! Does it mean he's into his *own* mother?"

"Shit. That *would* be gnarly."

"I don't think so. I can't really picture it."

María Inés was a kindly, generous woman. Brought home-made baked goods when she came to visit. Often still warm from the oven.

But in terms of her appearance—speaking strictly physically—she wasn't your typical object of feminine beauty. Wide to the point of morbid obesity, with one of those double stomachs that pooched out over the crotch. Also, on one cheek she had a large port-wine stain. In the shape of Italy, weirdly. The first time he'd noticed, he'd thought it might be a tattoo.

Couldn't ask, more's the pity.

Also, her hair was thinning. Patches of scalp showing through.

They hadn't met the father yet. He was a seasonal worker, away in the Central Valley picking fruit. Strawberries or grapes. Amy had once remarked that considering Luis's mother, and then Luis, the dad must look like a movie star.

Buzz had felt bad. His wife could be, on occasion, cruel.

"It isn't her fault," he'd said. "Maybe she has a skin condition. Not everyone has the money for dermatologists. Or maybe she's just not vain. And has other priorities. Such as taking care of her children."

Amy was penitent after that remark.

"You know what they say," he said now. "The heart wants what the heart wants."

"It's not the *heart*, Buzz."

"Ha *ha*."

"So what are you going to do?"

"What *can* I do?"

"He needs to seek counseling."

"Counseling? For a MILF fetish?"

"But it's not *MILFs*, Buzz. You said it yourself! It's wrinkled old hags!"

"Well. *Hags* is, maybe, overly negative."

"This is about our daughter's happiness!"

"I mean. Is it *harmful*?"

"Maybe not now. But it *could* be."

"I don't know. A shrink seems punitive. Like Christians trying to force their kids not to be gay. Sending them off to straight camp for a homophobic brainwashing. Causing teen suicides."

"It's not the same."

"It isn't?"

"Buzz! No! What if he cheats on her with a senior citizen?"

He hadn't considered that. Admittedly.

He preferred not to picture it. Shook his head, as if to dislodge a cobweb.

"You *know* what we agreed," said Amy sternly. "We went all in, getting behind their impulsive child marriage, on *one* condition, which was she had to have that implant put into her arm so she can finish college before there's any new additions to the *family*!"

She was speeding up as she went along. Gathering momentum, verbally.

"But what does that have to do with—"

"We've done so *much* for him! Been *so* supportive! But with the granny porn, all bets are off! What if he's in there having sick fantasies about, like, your *mother*? He *met* her, you know. At the home. And now that I think of it, he was *extremely* deferential."

"Jesus! He's not having sex fantasies about my aged mother."

"It's so disturbing. Like necrophilia. Buzz, I'm *serious*. That boy needs therapy."

At first he fully intended to take up the matter with Luis. As his wife had ordered him. For a day or two that was his honest intention.

He'd hang around the rec room after Amy and Liza went to bed, making small talk and waiting to feel a vibe where he could broach the subject.

But he never felt the vibe. The vibe was a total no-show.

And Luis was polite about the small talk, but always waiting to get to work. So Buzz would nurse his beer till it was gone, then pad in his sock feet up to the bedroom.

He realized he didn't have the stones for it. The cojones! The balls he possessed were not up to the task they'd been given.

So he made excuses for his evasion. Amy was often right, but she was wrong on this one. Had a knee-jerk distrust of porn. For her, it wasn't a turn-on but an act of oppression. Understandable.

Yet at the same time, in her case, a Protestant hangover.

Making Luis talk to a shrink about his cougar scenarios would be *exactly* like the homophobic Christians.

Instead, what he did was buy the kid a MacBook.

When Amy found out, due to Luis's expressing his gratitude in a heartfelt way over the dinner table—with superlatives like "the most generous gift I've ever received"—he lightly, by implication, fibbed.

"So did the Zoom consult get set up?" she pressed later. "With the counselor? Before you went ahead and made this purchase?"

He inclined his head in a way that might, if you chose to interpret it that way, be seen as assent.

It wasn't a *nod*, as such. More of a friendly compromise between no and yes.

"It's all good," he said.

He *did* feel guilty about the deception, though. In the past, when he'd lied to Amy, it had been for her own protection. Say, when she asked about her upper-arm fat and he said, "No, dear, you don't have bingo wings. And they don't flap."

Or, "No, you weren't *that* rude to the underpaid customer-service representative you just spoke to on the phone from Hyderabad. You were defending your rights as a consumer!"

But in this case, the person he was protecting was himself. And his small testicles, like wrinkly prunes.

Also, he reasoned, he was protecting Luis, and by extension Liza. Confrontations over a porn habit were *not* the path to family cohesion.

But what he also felt was curious.

Initially he viewed his investigations of the granny videos as anthropological in nature. Educated curiosity.

In the end, though, porn was porn. Some of the old girls weren't bad at all. And they only had ten or fifteen years on *him*.

The uncomfortable part of the investigations was the awareness that he and Luis might be doing the same thing. In real time, he had to shunt away the awareness of their porn camaraderie.

If he didn't, the session would be wasted. A nonstarter.

Afterward, he'd shake his head at his own treachery. Good thing that was the last time, he'd tell himself. He only did it when he was alone in the house, with the doors locked and the security armed.

However.

He went into the den on a Wednesday, meaning to watch a bike race, and found Liza sitting in front of the desktop. Her laptop was updating, she said. And she had to keep looking for an apartment in Oakland. The one they'd picked before had been rented right out from under them. It was a housing *emergency*.

In a few weeks, she and Luis would be leaving for Berkeley.

He was alarmed. The sheer proximity of his daughter to the browser history. Couldn't remember if he'd cleared the cache the night before. No memory of it, one way or the other.

Probably, he told himself, gazing at her back nervously as he held the TV remote, it would turn out to be like one of those moments where, driving away from your house in the morning, you're sure you've left a stove burner on. You turn around and drive back.

But sure enough, you'd switched it off after all.

He told himself to relax. Enjoy the Gran Piemonte.

Liza squealed.

"Oh my God! Dad! *Dad!* It autofilled a porn site! Look! A naked lady!"

He closed his eyes for a second.

The burner *was* still on.

"You know what that *means*, right? This site has already been visited! On *this* computer!"

She swiveled in her chair and faced him.

Stay calm. Indifferent. No dog in the fight.

He leaned forward, pretending to be focused on the race.

"*What*, now? Pornography?"

Stole a quick glance at her. Her eyes were large and round.

"Dad! This is disgusting! Nicky's been down here watching *cougar* porn!"

But Nick never used the old desktop—had two better computers in his room. A high-end gaming PC and a Mac. Still, to argue against it . . . Also, he couldn't out Luis.

That would be low. Considering.

"Well, heck, it's not against the law, Liza," he said, shrugging. "You need to stop policing your big brother. He's a grown person."

"But Dad! It's the *family* computer! And now I'm being *assaulted* by these misogynistic images! It's practically gender-based *harassment*!"

"*Is* it, though?"

"Yes! It totally *is*!"

"OK. Well. In due time, you will recover from the trauma. Now. Can I please watch the race in peace? Before it's over?"

"Dad. You know I've been easing up on Nicky. Right? Have you even *noticed*? But this crosses the line. It's not OK. It is *literally* a form of psychic violence."

He leaned back on the couch and closed his eyes again.

Gen Z, at times, was exhausting.

"You need to talk to him. You need to *confront* him. And tell him he can't watch porn down here. I'm serious, Daddy."

He opened his eyes. Light at the end of the tunnel. A way out.

"So you want *me* to talk to him? About the porn?"

"Yes, Dad! You *have* to! *I* can't do it. He won't listen to me. He'll sneer and say I'm overreacting."

"I tell you what," said Buzz. "I'll have a chat with him. As long as you promise me: you *do not* bring it up yourself. With him or anyone else. I don't want your mother or Luis involved. They have enough to deal with. And Nicky's already getting a lot of pressure. To change up his job situation. *I'll* handle it. Discreetly. Do I have your word?"

"Fine."

She turned back around and tap-tapped at the keyboard.

The naked lady went away.

Phew. Dodged a bullet.

No. Dodged a hand grenade.

"Oh," she said. "Dad. What's the monthly budget, again? For me and Luis's apartment?"

Seamlessly switching gears. Like someone who wasn't traumatized in the least.

"I don't have the figure committed to memory, sweetheart. It's on the spreadsheet. You can bring it up in Excel."

Women entrusted you with the difficult work of wrangling other men.

And usually, you opted not to. A smart man knew the wisdom in avoiding conflicts with others of his kind.

Still, it had been a come-to-Jesus moment. Where he realized the shared computer was the stupidest way he could possibly have chosen.

He'd wanted to avoid using his work laptop. In case the IT guys were spying on him. So he'd doubled down on Luis's mistake.

Moronic. Never again.

But he also recognized he'd been lying to Amy about something else. To her *and* to himself.

He had to come clean.

"Listen," he said to her that weekend, after they'd messed around. "You know the deal with the foot pain? Where I chickened out? Of that race in the Sierras?"

She nodded.

"So yeah, that wasn't the reason."

"It wasn't?"

"No. It's that . . . it's my knee, Amy. It's gotten so bad."

His leg joints were giving out. One knee was worse than the other, but there was a hip problem too. The sports medicine guy and the osteopath had both said it: if he wanted to keep running, he'd have to have the left knee replaced. Probably, in a couple of years, the right. Eventually, his hips.

And what they counseled was, he shouldn't do it.

Instead, he should stop running marathons. Even half-marathons. Even the piddling 5Ks he used to make fun of.

Probably altogether.

"Oh," said Amy. She lay looking at him, propped up on an elbow. "*Now* I get it. I was wondering why you'd slowed down so much. On the training."

"You know what they want me to do? Yoga! And swimming. Old-codger shit."

"I'm so sorry."

"It's been . . . it's a hard pill to swallow."

"It has to be. I know how much you love it."

"Yeah. Where am I gonna get my adrenaline rushes in the future?"

"You'll figure out something. Running's not the only way."

"But it was *my* only way."

She leaned over and kissed him. "At least you're still good in the sack."

"Huh. The clock's ticking on that one, too."

"Never."

She said never. But he had a sinking feeling.

The mothers were throwing a party for Liza and Luis's send-off. It would be at their house—bigger, with a backyard—and he and Amy would foot the bill, but María Inés would do the cooking.

He didn't pay much attention. The party was set for a Saturday, and they were leaving Sunday: he and Amy were going to drive them up to Berkeley. So while the women were stringing up festive lighting and bustling around with food, he was helping to pack and load the car. Liza filled the boxes, Buzz taped them up, and Luis carried them down to the garage.

On top of one box was the large stuffed rabbit she'd slept with her arms around since she was two. Even when Luis was in the bed. If that didn't make a mockery of her being, as she declared, a "married woman," he didn't know what did. One day, when she was oversleeping, he'd knocked, pushed the bedroom door open, and seen the three of them spooned. Luis's arms around her and her arms around Bunny.

"Married." And still clutching her stuffed animal.

Just as a body pillow, she'd claimed. A good shape.

The rabbit lay on its side on a cushion of folded clothes atop the box, long, floppy ears extended.

Those ears were soft. Despite many washings, not as white as they used to be.

Bunny'd gone gray over the years. Like him.

"I can't believe Bunny's leaving."

"Dad. That's psychologically transparent."

"It is?"

"You mean me, right? You can't believe *I'm* leaving. Bunny's an inanimate object."

"Wow. That's pretty cold, Liza. After so many years of service."

"My dad's a sucker for Bunny," she told Luis. "A bleeding heart. One time I got mad at him and threw her. He kneeled down and picked her up like a baby. He was all, Oh, don't feel sad, Bunny. She didn't mean to hurt you."

Luis smiled. "Hey. I get that."

"Some things have *character*," said Buzz.

He felt confused, but also had a conviction. Wanted to explain it, but it wasn't simple.

"Especially stuffed animals. They don't have to be *living*. There's this, you know, *force field* around them. What they've received. And what they've given."

His daughter was staring at him.

"Something that's *held* so much," he said, struggling. "Something that's *loved*. Its history . . . I don't know. Kind of *emanates* from it. Maybe you say you *don't* love Bunny. Maybe you say love isn't the right word. Because she's not *real*. Like in *The Velveteen Rabbit* . . . remember? I read it to you a hundred times. You were obsessed with it when you were little. But Bunny *is* real. Not alive, but still real. She doesn't just *remind* us of our memories. It's more than that. She *embodies* them. Those times that can never be repeated. All bundled up in her soft body."

He couldn't make them understand. How once-beloved objects rippled their essences into the air between people.

How humble things were made precious by feeling.

"Anyway," she said, "I'm not taking Bunny, Dad."

He gazed at her. Blinking.

"You're not even *taking* her?"

"There's no room."

He put his hand on Bunny. Some of her seams were fraying. She was being abandoned.

"There's plenty of *room*," he said. "You have a whole apartment."

"In the *car*, Dad. We don't have room in the *car*."

"We can *make* room," he muttered.

"Dad," said Liza gently. She put a hand on his arm. "Hey. *Daddy*. Don't cry."

What? Cry?

There was water on his bottom lids. He brushed it away.

"Oh. Yes. No! Sorry. Ridiculous."

A sentimental old fool. That was how she saw him.

"I guess it *is* pretty transparent," he said.

Still, when Luis went downstairs with the next box, Liza picked up Bunny and looked at her face. The large, dark eyes.

Ran her fingers along an ear.

"Listen," she said. "She's too fragile to travel. You see this leg? It's almost off. I already sewed it up three times. So I have to leave her here. But I'll check on her whenever I come home. And I want you to take care of her for me. Don't let Mom, like, clean up my room and throw her out. *Ever.* Do you promise?"

There were more guests than he'd expected. Christmas lights decorated the trees. All across the backyard, on the ground, sat small brown paper bags with votives flickering in them.

Fire hazards, said the dad part of him. They should have used those LED candles.

Let it go, killjoy, rebuked the other parts.

Music playing.

He knew some of them. Liza's high-school crowd. Nick's fantasy role-playing pals, each one a bona fide nerd. If there was a certification for the title, they'd hold diplomas. With honors.

But a lot of the guests he'd never met before. Luis's cousins, uncles, and aunts. María Inés's longtime neighbors from Encinitas.

With a few beers under his belt, he wandered among the groups. A solitary pilgrim. Making his own journey.

He picked up snatches of conversation.

"*Her?* She believes in *everything.* You know what she believed in? Back in the day? Bonsai Kittens."

". . . but why *him?* Where do they see the charisma? The face pout? The bad hair? That lifts up in the breeze like a toupee? And the suits look cheap, but that's because he has them tailored with giant shoulders. To hide his body shape."

". . . growing kittens in jars?"

"He's just such an *obvious* monster. And you know what he was afraid of? Getting hit by fruit. Or pies. The leader of the free world. Afraid of flying fruit."

"When the Lord closes a door, He opens a window."

"This friend I have? She makes me doubt my reality. And not in a good way, either."

"But who wants to climb through a window? Here's *my* question. Why doesn't the Lord open another door?"

Sometimes he stopped and spoke a word or two, sometimes he said nothing and kept walking.

Hell, maybe he could start to walk more. Now that he couldn't run. Walk for days. Walk for weeks. An old man, weary but wise from his travels. Walk toward the far horizon, where the sun was going down.

For the moment, though, he walked holding a beer.

Walking and drinking, he cast across the garden, over the guests, a benediction of fondness.

Intangible, sure. But truly meant.

Tonight all of our paths are crossing, he told them silently.

And from this day till the last day, they will never cross again.

ARTIST

So-called conspiracies, she told the girls, were not created equal. Hillary Clinton sucking the bone marrow from infants as part of a liberal cabal, while also molesting them, should not be placed in the same category with mountains of factual evidence that multinationals like DuPont, Dow, and Bayer routinely manufactured, and aggressively marketed, neurotoxic chemicals and endocrine disruptors that poisoned public waters, killed off insect pollinators, and gave diseases like Parkinson's to impoverished farmworkers.

Sure, one might be called a theory, if you defined *theory* not as a hypothesis that could be tested but as a paranoid class-war fantasy.

The other was a fact.

"But Mom," said Mia, "is something a *conspiracy* if it just happens because of, like, capitalism?"

"Yes, dear," Helen told her. "If there's collaboration. And malice aforethought. *You* two only believe in a corporate conspiracy once someone's made a movie about it."

Shelley sided with her sister. "If you call it a *conspiracy*, Mother," she'd lecture, "you lose all credibility. You're a Marjorie Taylor Greene. Or an Alex Jones. But from the left. Avoid the *word*. It's basic messaging. Say 'coordinated campaign.' Or 'calculated disinformation program.' The second you say *conspiracy*, you're a wack job."

"So you want me to speak in euphemisms."

"It's *not* a euphemism. It's just more specific."

"For genocide, do you prefer 'targeted ethnic mass-extermination effort'?"

"Well. Not *effort*. It has to be successful. By definition."

"Successful. A *successful* extermination."

"You know what I mean, Mom. Not an *effort*. An outcome. Like, a result."

Shelley was sharp as a tack. But she was all about the spin. Drawn to image and manipulation like a moth to the flame.

Somewhere, raising her girls, Helen had taken a wrong turn. Left out the part about morality.

She'd been too busy, as a single mother, making lunches and driving them to extracurricular activities.

If Michael had lived and the girls had two parents, maybe it would have gone better.

Shelley could still use her talents for good. She was only twenty-three. But *would* she?

Doubtful. She liked the game of selling. And getting paid to play it. In sales you had to understand desire. Not only how to satisfy it, but how to create it in the first place.

That was how she rhapsodized about her career path. Sitting at the kitchen island and doodling on an iPad with her finger as Helen made them cocktails. One of her Friday-night visits.

"You're catering to the *id*," Helen had said. "What if major talent agencies like yours tried to transform the collective? Wouldn't that be more of a challenge? Wouldn't it be less like shooting fish in a barrel?"

"The collective doesn't have an agent, Mom."

"But instead of trying to place actors in movies and shows that promote the status quo, the same as a zillion that have come before, you could try to place them in projects with a progressive agenda."

"You know what that would be? A failure. Your theory of change is, like, basically nonexistent."

"You should watch *Manufacturing Consent*. Or even read it."

"Of *course* I've seen it. Communications 101. I was a *freshman*."

"You didn't take it to heart, obviously."

"Mom. Noam Chomsky's a dinosaur. And not even a ferocious *T. rex*, either. More of a brontosaurus. A lumbering plant-eater."

She drew a picture. A vaguely Chomsky-like head, with glasses, on a long neck. Then four squat legs.

And a tiny tail. Like a giraffe's.

"You really don't know your brontosauruses."

"Here's what I *do* know, Mom. Those screenplays with what you call a *progressive* agenda? They're mostly super bad. Earnest and lame. Unless you can attach a star who's into, like, liberal vanity projects. But the market can only take so many Ruffalos."

"What's a ruffalo? Is it like a buffalo?"

Shelley snickered. "Kind of."

"What we need isn't more hacks. We need a Leni Riefenstahl of the left."

"A Nazi propagandist. That's what you want me to be?"

"A brilliant propagandist. But in the service of the *people*."

"That's exactly what Hitler said. No *doubt*. When he was pitching her to take the gig."

"Well. If you don't know the difference between a genocidal tyrant and the common good, I guess we can stop talking."

"Yeah. And start drinking. You've been mixing those margaritas for ten minutes."

Like banging your head against a wall.

Mia was taking a gap year before she went to college, claiming she'd use it to "find her bliss."

Helen couldn't tell if that was ironic. Or if Mia had actually, at some point, familiarized herself with the writings of Joseph Campbell. But she'd agreed to it.

Partly, avoiding the empty nest. When she'd have to start using dating apps. Or take up knitting. Possibly both.

Did Mia have any ideas? she asked. About the bliss?

"The field is totally open," said Mia. "Radical openness. That's the beauty of it."

So—not even a shortlist?

"Something with kittens and puppies? Or I could help save koalas. They're *so cute*, Mom. And lots of them are burning up. Plus dying from chlamydia."

"Shut *up*!" said Shelley. "Are *not*!"

"Google it. Or maybe I could do fundraising for unfairly canceled celebrities. Like Aziz Ansari? That was mega sad."

"But he wasn't *fully* canceled, was he?" asked Shelley.

"Huh. I'm not sure, TBH."

"That whole thing was bullshit."

"Garbage. I had worse dates in junior *high*."

"As usual, I don't know who you're talking about," said Helen, but they ignored her.

"Or maybe I could get into influencing. *I* could influence, right? I'm OK pretty. Or I could do unboxing videos. Or pole dancing."

"But not that last one, though, maybe," said Helen.

"It's not all about *stripping* these days, Mom. It's fitness. I took two classes, remember? The lady said I was a natural."

"Even so. Pole dancing's not a college major."

Mia had to volunteer, was the agreement they'd made. For at least twenty-five hours a week. To increase her chances of bliss-finding.

She started out at an animal shelter, pursuing puppies and kittens, but it turned out not to be a no-kill shelter. So she came home crying after two days. Locked herself in her room listening to music. On the family Spotify account there were songs about untimely death.

Volunteer opportunities weren't what they used to be, for high-school graduates. When Helen was young, you could volunteer for the Dalai Lama himself with a high-school education. Practically.

Or a congressman, anyway.

Now the pickings were slim. They wanted an impressive résumé, even when you worked for free.

"Look," she said to Mia, after the animal-shelter trauma. Scrolling through offerings at the kitchen island. "Here's one taking Meals on Wheels to the elderly. It'd be better than the pet shelter. They don't euthanize old people, at least."

"Just a matter of time," said Shelley. "Look at the Netherlands. And Belgium. Anyway, old people are depressing."

"*You're* depressing," said Helen. "Jesus!"

"It's not my bliss," said Mia firmly.

"You *do* realize that jobs are work, right?" asked Helen.

"Not necessarily."

"No, typically, they are. Ask anyone."

"*Your* job isn't work."

"That's because I'm an artist."

"See? Exactly."

"You should do the Peace Corps, Mia," said Shelley. "Sign up to build a septic tank in a poor community."

"Too late for that," said Helen. "She would have had to apply about a year ago."

"Also, no," said Mia.

"Let me guess," said Helen. "Septic tanks aren't your bliss."

"Mia's problem," said Shelley, popping an olive into her mouth, "is that she thinks volunteering should involve decorating cup-cakes, wearing a hot outfit, and giving out teddy bears."

"Exactly! Mom. What combines those?"

"Being an idiot?"

"Mom. Seriously."

Candy striping came to mind. Did it exist, these days? Vague pictures in her head of women in pink costumes, handing out balloons to cancer children.

"Maybe you need to think about this differently. Decide what you'd like to do, then figure out where there's a need for it. How it could help others. Without a massive infusion of cash from me. We can't give out hundreds of teddy bears."

"So like, invent my own charity?"

"I don't know about charity, per se. But *start* something. Your own service project."

"*Mother*," said Shelley, "that's not a terrible idea."

"Yeah, no," said Mia. "It doesn't totally suck."

"High praise indeed."

An older neighbor, often crotchety, came over that Saturday to talk about what she called "the lawnmower problem."

The lawnmower problem, as she saw it, was noise.

Helen's work had wound down for the day, and Miss Caroline, as the girls had always called her, was lonely. So Helen invited her into the kitchen and brewed a cup of Earl Grey. Since Miss Caroline didn't partake of spirits anymore.

She began hauling herself creakily onto a tall counter stool. "These things weren't made for people with bursitis."

Helen apologized, saying they could sit somewhere else, but it was too late: the feat had been achieved. Miss Caroline was perched.

"As soon as Lewis turns off his mower, it's the weedwacker. Then, two hours later, just when I've sat down next to my lilacs for a pleasant *déjeuner sur l'herbe*, the Sturgetts bring out *their* mower. It's running *now*! You can't hear it from here. But the racket is just *constant*!"

"Oh, I know."

"And I like to be in my *garden*! It's my happy place. It's why I even *live* on this block. Those mowers are the *bane* of my existence. Just no tranquility. You can't even sit there and listen to the wind moving the trees, on the weekends. It's just, mow, mow, mow!"

"Hey there, Miss Caroline," said Mia, bounding in on her large, spongy sneakers and making for the fridge.

"Hello, my dear. I like your ponytail."

"Oh, thank you!"

"The mowing needs to be coordinated," Caroline told Helen. "On a *schedule*. There should be noisy hours. And quiet ones."

"Why don't you bring it up with the neighborhood association?"

"I can't! They do it all on the *computers*. They don't even have real *meetings* anymore."

"They use an app," said Helen.

Caroline frowned.

"Miss Caroline. Do you have a smartphone?" asked Mia, pouring herself a lemonade.

"Oh . . . it's probably smart?" She fumbled in a pocket and brought out an iPhone. With a case like a rubber tank. "My grandson got it for me. He makes me carry it everywhere. In case of an emergency. He can *see* where it *is*!"

"Amazing," nodded Helen.

Mia sat down on the stool next to her. "Is it OK if I mess around with it?"

"Certainly, dear. The secret code is 1111."

"Mom. What's the name of that neighborhood app?"

Helen went to her purse and consulted her own phone. Mia installed the app, then brought it up.

"What's an app?" asked Miss Caroline.

"It's like a card! You play bridge, right?"

"I do enjoy bridge. And spades."

"Think of an app like a card. But you have to grab it to play it. And this here, called the App Store, is the deck."

"Oh! OK."

"Let's set you up with your own account. Then you can tell them what you think about the mowing!"

"Oh, I don't *know*. I don't have my readers on me."

"Try mine," said Helen, removing them from her face.

"I promise! It's so *easy*! Here. I'll put it in for you. What do you want your username to be?"

"A user name?"

"Like, your handle. What you go by. You could use your real name or go with a nickname. That just the other users see. On this one app. Maybe ironic. Say, RadBikerChick. Or edgy. Like, SluttyGrandma."

Miss Caroline giggled.

Helen could *not* have pulled that one off.

Watching her daughter slowly, patiently going through the steps, she felt proud.

After that Mia was out of the house more. She went to the condo of a friend's grandmother, where she showed the grandmother how to use social media to look at pictures of distant family.

Then she went to see the grandfather, who lived in a care facility. When he showed other residents his new group-messaging app, and how they could all text each other in real time from different parts of the building, she was suddenly in demand. Moving from one assisted-living apartment to the next.

What the deal was, she said, was old people owned these devices, which in a lot of cases their kids or grandkids had foisted on them. But often those kids never took the time to walk them through it.

"Just handed that shit over and then exited," said Mia. "You're welcome."

Or sometimes the old folks had bought the devices themselves but never learned how to use them.

All she did was set them up, she said. Made it so they could press the buttons. And a whole *world* was open to them.

"They're not depressing you too much?" asked Helen. "They're not exactly koalas."

"Holy shit, Mom. They might as *well* be. They're a handful. Those old folks *party*. I mean, depends what tier they're in, there's some that don't party anymore. But this one old biddy, Lucy? I saw the photos—she used to be, like, super hot. But even now, she *literally* has three boyfriends. And they don't even *know* about each other."

"You could monetize this gig," said Shelley, admiring.

"It's a *service* project, Shelley," said Helen.

"It wouldn't be fun if I charged for it," said Mia. "I like to *give* them something."

"You just like being *liked*," scoffed Shelley. "Your 'service project' is a bid for popularity."

"So what, Shelley?" shrugged Mia. "It's better to be popular than to be a dick."

On the neighborhood app Miss Caroline posted a painstakingly edited paragraph about peace, listening to the sounds of nature, such as birds, and what she called the "blessed oasis of retirement" being turned into a "Monster Truck rally of roaring mechanical noise." She made a plea for kindness.

In the form of a coordinated lawnmowing schedule.

One neighbor wrote hastily, with spelling errors and a few sad-face emojis, that she just couldn't handle any more *rules*.

"We don't *have* any rules," Helen remarked. "But whatever."

Another said it could lead to longer grass. If they couldn't mow at the prescribed times. Not *everyone* was retired. Some of us had to work for a living, he wrote.

Mia went over to Miss Caroline's house to help her with more apps. Apps to talk to town councilors and apps for the public library.

But Miss Caroline was trembling, she said. Almost teary. There wasn't civic duty anymore, she'd told Mia. There wasn't decency.

"Isn't there anything we can do?" asked Mia.

Part of the problem was, said Mia, the ageism thing. Plus sexism! The neighbors ignored Miss Caroline because she was an old woman.

"And, if we're being honest, a bit crabby," added Helen.

"But she's not wrong," said Mia. "It *is* annoying. I never noticed it when I was in school. But it's how the whole *block* sounds. If I leave my window open, for fresh air overnight, I'm woken up at six."

"You know what she needs? An ambassador."

"Ambassador?"

"An OK pretty, young ambassador."

Mia cocked her head, considering.

"It's the husbands that do the mowing, right?"

"One or two households have yard guys, I think. But mostly, yeah. It's pretty gendered. Sons and husbands."

"So the question is, who the deciders are. Is it them? Or is it the partners? Wives and mothers? Like telling them to do it?"

"Tough call," said Helen. "But my money's on the women."

She'd had a lawn, way back when. Eventually she'd replaced it with a xeriscape setup, rocks and low-water shrubs and flowers. One reason, probably, that Caroline had chosen her to complain to. *She* wasn't doing any mowing. She was blameless.

But when they first moved in, when the girls were very little and Michael was still alive, there'd been some grass in front. She had a hazy memory of a mower in the garage. And of nagging him.

Felt the old tug of remorse, as it occurred to her. If she'd known what a brief time he had, how quickly he would cease to be, she would have skipped the nagging. Entirely.

There was a lot she would have skipped. If she had known.

And even more she would have *done*.

Shown him she knew how good he was. She would have fawned over him.

Her remorse had receded, over the fifteen years since he died. But sometimes it rushed back.

In a swift fold. A buckling of her stomach.

The pinch of nearly forgotten love.

It was late in the year for an ice cream social, Mia agreed. But it was still so *warm* out. These days September could pass for August.

"An ice cream social?" said Helen.

Where did she get this stuff? A movie from the fifties?

"It can't be cocktails," said Mia, "because I'm not old enough and it wouldn't be wholesome."

One family was Mormon, one was straightedge . . . she didn't know everyone's deal, but plus, there were probably AA people. It had to be outside. During the day.

"And a barbecue is too much work," said Mia. "All that meat, ick. And women have sweet tooths. More than men."

"Is that a fact?" asked Helen.

"Ice cream social sounds feminine," said Mia. "So a lot of the men won't come. Saul and Steven might show up, because they're fun, but they have a gardener. He comes on Tuesdays."

She went door to door with invitations. Made them look extra-feminine.

Also, she didn't want to offend Miss Caroline, but it was best she didn't attend. So she made sure it was a day when Miss Caroline was off on a visit to her grandson.

Helen kept working on a late commission while Mia borrowed extra coolers and folding chairs and filled the freezer with ice cream. When she emerged from her studio at the appointed hour the backyard was frilly with paper decorations. Tables were placed in the shade of the patio, covered in cloths and coolers full of ice. Bowls of colorful sprinkles and sundae sauces.

Guests wandered in through their side gate, following the cheerful signs with arrows and pictures of ice cream. Sure enough, mostly women. A couple of older bachelors. And Saul and Steven, from three doors down, brought their fluffy white dog. He wheeled around in circles, nipping at people's heels, till they gave him a piece of rawhide in the shape of a pretzel. Then he settled down at their feet and gnawed on it.

Mia, her hair in pigtails, wore a pinafore-type sundress that made her look about twelve. She'd enlisted two friends to help scoop up the ice cream.

In the background, music played softly.

Chamber music, Helen realized. Which Mia never listened to.

And right on cue, as they were settling down to eat their ice cream and talking, a mower started up. Next door. Drowned out the chamber music and the conversation.

The next-door neighbor woman, Elise, looked sheepish. It was her husband mowing.

"Oh! That reminds me!" said Mia, clapping her hands. She ran over to the end of the ice cream table and grabbed a clipboard.

"I know, old-school," she told the first person she took it over to. "I'll write your name for you. So you don't have to put down your sundae. That looks *so* yummy. Caramel is my favorite. Oh, and your cell number. There are two slots, Saturday and Sunday.

Anytime between ten and twelve in the morning. Before it gets hot, or anything. I figure, it'll be more important in the spring. But there's still a little left of the season."

The person—Helen didn't even know her name; she lived far down on the corner—nodded with her mouth full.

"Can you spell it for me? I'm such a terrible speller . . . Oh, and I'll put it up on the app later, so everyone can see it. And so you don't forget, you'll even get a notification. It'll ping you! Like, Hey, it's mowing time! It's a surprise for Miss Caroline. You know, she's been feeling so bad lately. This'll cheer her up."

"We'll sign up too," said Steven. "We can change our guy to Saturday. Right, Saul?"

"We can absolutely change our guy."

"Also, what I like is, it'll be kind of a community activity," said Mia. "Everyone out there in their yards! At the same time! Like, waving to each other!"

Elise from next door wanted to look at Helen's work. A studio tour, she called it.

At first Helen skipped over the request and changed the subject, but she kept asking. In an encouraging voice, as though, by expressing her interest, she was flattering her. As though Helen silently yearned for the gift of her random next-door neighbor's interest. And should be grateful for it.

Elise, she strongly suspected, was a Republican. Her front-yard flowers were Day-Glo orange geraniums and gaudy impatiens that looked plastic. Arranged in symmetrical formations.

Aesthetics *were* politics, after all.

Also, she used Roundup on her weeds. Which included native wildflowers. Had the yard guy go around using a back-pack sprayer. Roundup and, even worse, imidacloprid—Helen had seen it in the bed of his truck. Compare-N-Save Insect Drench. A neonic, she happened to know. Pure poison.

No butterflies alighted on *her* blooms. And if they did make that mistake, they probably flitted off afterward to die.

"OK," said Helen finally. She was restless in her plastic chair. With her empty ice cream bowl tipped over beside her on the grass. "I can take you in, but don't feel you have to comment. There's no pressure for you to say you like anything."

"Oh, I know I *will*!" said Elise.

Say you like? thought Helen. Or like?

So she led her through the studio door. Thinking she should have poured herself a drink first. But booze didn't go well with ice cream. And it was too early anyway.

There were a couple of half-finished commissions on easels—one of an actress, one of a drummer in some band who'd insisted on posing with his Grammy behind him—and Elise stopped at the actress.

"I *recognize* her!" she said.

"Oh, uh-huh?" said Helen.

"She was in the movie about—wait, was it the one where they kidnap her son? Or . . ."

"I don't know, honestly," said Helen.

"No, wait. It was the one where the husband's a superspy. Or no! A killer. And she's a killer too. They don't even know the other one's a killer!"

Helen strolled ahead to the part of the room where she did her personal painting. Celebrity portraits were her bread and butter, but every day she did an hour or two of abstract work. Didn't show it much. But it was why she painted.

Michael had loved what she did. She'd just been making a name for herself when the girls were little. Then she'd done a painting of a famous friend's face on a whim—her only famous friend, at the time. Not quite ironic but playful, with a hint of caricature. After it had been hanging on her friend's dining room wall for two years, a snapshot had suddenly gone viral. And other famous people had piled on, offering generous sums for portraits of their own.

Michael hadn't wanted her to take commissions. You don't have to prostitute yourself, he had said. We'll get by.

And maybe they would have. But he'd died.

"What's this one of?" asked Elise, joining her in front of one of the abstracts.

"Oh, it's not really *of*," said Helen.

Elise nodded, not understanding, and cocked her head. Like she was wondering if the piece was sideways.

"That other one looks just *like* her, though," she said. "The movie star. Did you do it from a photo?"

After the guests had left, Helen sat in the backyard with Mia and her two girlfriends. They scrolled on their phones with empty white chairs scattered around them. Cartons of leftover ice cream slowly melting on the table.

She should take them to the freezer. A waste.

But she didn't move.

"I have to hand it to you. You're a schemer," she told Mia.

"It's a conspiracy," grinned Mia. "A conspiracy of me!"

In her grin Helen saw, for a second, a ghostly hint of Michael. His fondness for all of them.

So strong it stopped her breath.

Then it was gone, and her daughter was herself again.

TERRORIST

Steven said it wasn't *serious* hate. Probably just some frustrated guy stuck in the closet. "Nothing to be afraid of," he told Saul.

"What do you mean, it isn't *serious* hate? Is there *funny* hate?"

"Comedians do it all the time," said Steven.

"Come on. This isn't funny."

Steven picked up the latest note. A crude drawing of one guy standing behind another, brandishing a penis that looked like a banana. With two eggs suspended from the end.

"It sort of is."

"It's just dumb."

"The rendering is clearly absurdist. With a gesture to Warhol."

"It's still hate, Steven. Whether the perp is confused or not. Gay, or as straight as Mitt Romney."

"You're trying to tell me Mitt Romney is *straight*?"

They should report it, Saul argued. It had been going on for weeks. In their mailbox, which they couldn't see from the front

windows because of an oleander hedge, there'd be a folded piece
of paper slipped in between the bills and junk.

Words like *Fags* and *Faggots* in large block letters.

And once, *You Freddie Mercury fuckers!*

Steven had laughed at that one, too.

"As if it's an *insult*," he said. "More like a Make-a-Wish!"

Saul didn't laugh. He used to enjoy scooping the mail out of
the box. Now it was like running a gauntlet.

"People get fired for less," he said. "It's a macroaggression."

"I tell you what," Steven suggested. "I'll put up a security camera. We already own one, part of a package deal with the smart
thermostat. I didn't feel like installing it. But there's an app. And
a motion-sensitive floodlight. If we angle it off the front of the
roof, I think we could have a view."

"So now we're going to surveil our neighbors? Because of some
homophobic jerk?"

"You know the cops won't do shit. They'll smirk, drive off, and
say the same words we already saw on the pieces of paper."

So Steven went up onto the roof, working his manly magic
with loud power tools, and Saul went out to take Bette Midler
for a walk.

Bette Midler wasn't that into walks. He preferred sitting on
laps. But it couldn't be helped. He was a dog.

While he was doing his business—squatting, trembling, and
looking so pathetic it still made Saul blush after two years of
walking him—an old Beamer trying to parallel park scraped the
rear bumper of the car in front of it.

As Saul scooped up the business in his plastic baggie, the driver
got out, cursing.

Shelley, one of his neighbors' daughters. She'd moved out after college but came back for dinner every week.

He'd always liked Shelley. She had attitude.

"Saul! Shit. Do you know whose car this is?"

"No idea."

Bette Midler strained at the lead, trying to mount Shelley's leg.

"That's rude, Bette Midler," said Shelley. "I'm being sexually assaulted by a tiny poodle."

"Off! So sorry. But he's a bichon frisé."

"I didn't know he was a boy dog."

"He doesn't like us to mention it."

"So how'd he get the name?"

"People assume we gave it to him. Because we're gay and it's Bette Midler. But we got him from a shelter and he already had the name. He was no spring chicken. So we didn't try to change it."

"Does it have a *mark*? The other car? What do *you* think?"

"Hmm. Maybe a *faint* mark?" said Saul. "But it might have already been there, too. I can't tell if it looks new."

"Argh, I can't tell *either*."

"Maybe just leave a note."

She pawed through her bag—a Badgley Mischka. Or a decent knockoff. Then threw up her hands. "I don't have a pen. Or paper! I could get them from my mom. But then I'll have to tell her why. And she already thinks I'm a bad driver."

Saul cocked his head. He couldn't help smiling.

"OK, fine," said Shelley. "I *am* a bad driver. Still. I have my pride."

"Of *course*. Come on, I can get you a pen and paper. Bette Midler wants to go in anyway."

"Oh, Steven's on the roof!" she said as they approached. "Huh. He looks good up there. Silhouetted. And holding that drill."

"He always looks good holding a drill."

"Aren't you afraid he'll fall?"

"You read my mind. I ideate. It's why I went on a dog walk."

"Steven! Don't fall off the roof!" called Shelley.

Steven saluted.

"Probably can't hear you. Hearing-impaired. From too many years of loud music."

He set the baggie down on the stoop and opened the door for her.

But instead of going in, she stood there on the steps. Seemed to be frozen in place. One hand resting on her bag's zipper.

"Shelley? Is something wrong?"

"Oh. Yeah. No. I was spacing. You know. My dad died in a fall."

"I'm sorry. I *didn't* know."

She went through the door.

"I don't remember it. Except for how it felt at the funeral. The people milling around in shock. Looking blank and stunned. Because he was in his thirties. Hiking in the Santa Monica Mountains with a friend. Just for a couple of hours, it was supposed to be. And then the side of the hill slid down and he broke his neck. They said erosion."

"I knew your father had died young. But I never heard how."

"His friend fell too, but he only broke some ribs. Anyway, so I always think about falling. When I see people in high places."

He closed the door behind them. Since the notes started, it felt like he was shutting out a malignant force field. Emanating from the mailbox.

"Of course you do. That's terrible, Shelley."

He was at a loss for words. After a few moments, leaned down and unclipped the leash.

Bette Midler instantly tried to hump Shelley's foot again.

"Off!" he said. "He doesn't do this, usually. He seems to have a thing for you."

"Maybe he smells my boyfriend's dog. It's a pit-boxer mix. And a public menace, honestly. If they were introduced, he would probably eat Bette Midler."

"Or he likes your boots. Bette Midler has impeccable taste."

"Ha ha. Thank you. I got them for sixty bucks on Depop."

"Let's see now, pen and paper . . . follow me."

There was blank paper on his drafting table, so he led her into the study. With the dog frolicking around their feet. One day Bette Midler would trip him.

On the table, also, were the notes from the box. Right on the top, the men with the banana penis between them.

Shelley caught sight of it. Hard to miss.

"That's a whole other story," he said.

"It doesn't look like your best work," she said. "Architects have to be good at drawing. Don't they?"

"Someone's been leaving them in the mailbox." He took a sheet of printer paper out of a tray and handed it over.

"Obscene pictures? In your mailbox?"

"And some like this," he said, and slid the banana-men off the pile so she could see the notes beneath. She peered down.

"Are you kidding?"

"I wish."

"Saul! Did you call the cops?"

"I don't think it's a crime. Unless there's the threat of violence."

"It isn't?"

"Well. Maybe the part where they're tampering with the mail."
He explained about the camera. Why Steven was up on the roof.
"I hope you catch the hater," she said as she left.

But the camera was overkill. It notified him whenever someone walked past. *Event: Person seen*, it pinged on his phone. Fifty times a day. And the nighttime footage didn't capture faces well.

He got into the habit of scrolling through the day's Events. Just as practice—they hadn't gotten any notes since the camera went in. He'd scroll while Steven watched a game.

Or YouTube tutorials on how to replace linoleum with cork flooring. Or fix up old motorcycles.

"Look, this is a Vincent," he said. "A Black Shadow."

He fantasized about rebuilding vintage motorcycles.

"But you don't *own* a Vincent Black Shadow."

"It's just interesting."

"Death traps."

"But I *could* have one, if I took a safety course. You said so when we got married. You promised."

"Yeah, theoretically," said Saul. "I wouldn't feel that great about it. But OK. Yes."

"I *could* have one," repeated Steven. Glassy-eyed and dreamy.

The Events showed neighbors walking past. Minding their own business.

The terrorist had gone to ground, said Steven. Hiding in a fox-hole. Like, back in the day, Saddam Hussein. Or was it Osama bin Laden.

Until.

"Look!" crowed Steven, coming in after work with the mail. He flapped a paper in the air. "Jackpot! Did you watch last night's footage yet?"

"I did! This morning. Nothing."

"So it must have been in broad daylight!" said Steven.

The note said *Man slut. Dick eater!*

"Man slut?" asked Steven. "It's singular? It's just one of us?"

"Must be talking about *you*. Personally, I was never promiscuous."

"Me either!"

"You *did* have that thing with Aldus. Where you broke up with him for the guy with the six-pack. That you'd already fooled around with."

"The steroid abuser? I was in my *twenties!*"

"Still. Maybe the hater knows all about it."

"He doesn't know *shit*. Bring up today's Events. I'm on the edge of my seat!"

Saul's eyes got tired as he clicked and scrolled.

"Wait! Wait! Right there! Go back."

"But that was Mia. It's not *Mia*."

Mia was a sweetheart. Shelley had an edge, but her little sister was all softness.

"Right after Mia. Didn't you see?"

He rewound a bit.

Mia passed the mailbox. Smoking a cigarette.

"Oh my God, *do not* tell her mother."

"I am not a snitch."

"It's probably just a joint."

"There! *There!*"

A blurry head. Low to the ground. Barely above the mailbox itself.

"What is it?" asked Steven. "A midget?"

"First off, don't say midget."

"Sorry."

"What I'd suggest is, it's a kid."

"He's standing there. He's reaching! Look, that's the mailbox flap opening!"

"The face is—I can't see the face."

"But damn. Damn. It's just a *little boy*."

The boy exited. Frame left.

They sat with it.

"A little kid," marveled Steven. "Huh."

"Maybe someone put him up to it."

"What if he doesn't even know what's *in* the notes? Because, you know, they're always folded."

"Yeah, but I'd open it and look. Wouldn't you?"

"Do you know any little kids on the block?"

"Let me think. There's the LDS folks, right? And then that new family. In the Craftsman bungalow. From Ethiopia? Who just moved in? The mother's lovely. I don't have their names down. I want to say, Amala? Amana? I don't know. She looks like David Bowie's widow. The supermodel."

"Iman."

They gazed at each other.

"Oh, *fuck*. It better not be a kid of color," said Saul.

"That would be so fucked."

"We couldn't call him on it."

"Then we'd be the gay racists."

"Even though your dad is black?"

"You *know* I always passed. I'd have to trot him out like a show pony. Like Dad, hey, fly out for a visit! We haven't seen you in ages! And can you hang around in the front yard a lot? Like a lawn jockey? So we can safely accuse a kid from Africa of being a homophobe?"

"It's probably the Mormons, anyway. They hate the gays."

"Not all of them."

"You definitely don't get your own planet after you die. If you're a fag."

"That's been discredited. Even the good Mormons don't get their own planet. It was just, like, misinformation from that musical. *The Book of Mormon*."

"And would a boy from Ethiopia know who Freddie Mercury *was*? So short. He looked like, grade-school age."

"I need a drink."

"And you deserve one."

They moved to the dining room bar. Bette Midler woke up from his nap and jumped off the couch, following.

Saul poured out gin.

"The good news is," said Steven, over his gimlet, "if it's just a kid, acting alone, there *is* nothing to be afraid of."

"You were right all along."

"But on the other hand, if there's someone else behind it . . ."

"If the kid's just the messenger?"

"It could still escalate. I guess."

"Wait," said Saul, excited. He set down his drink, splashing a bit, and grabbed Steven's arm. "*Mia* was in the video. Just a few feet ahead of him!"

"Right! She could have *seen* him," said Steven.

"I'll text her."

"Maybe face-to-face is better."

"Let's take Bette Midler over. She likes to visit with him."

"He has crushes on both those girls. Even though she did say, that one time, that she wished he was a fawn-colored pug. They're her favorite."

"It stung, but he got over it."

So they leashed up Bette Midler and took a stroll.

At Mia and Helen's house no one was answering the door. But they could hear voices from the backyard, so they went around the side. Called over the gate.

Mia came running over. Perfect skin. And bright-blue mascara on her long eyelashes. Reminded Saul of dragonflies.

Behind her, people in costumes were flailing around with swords.

"Oh my," said Saul. "What's this, an amateur theatrical?"

"My friend's brother's LARPing group. Doing fighter practice, I guess? They got kicked out of the park so I said they could use our place. I'd ask you in, but you don't want to see this. Seriously." She lowered her voice. "I've only been watching for five minutes but I can already tell—I won't be able to unsee it."

"You poor thing," said Steven, shaking his head. "No good deed goes unpunished."

"We won't stay long," said Saul. "We just have a quick question for you. So earlier today, you walked past our house, right? And there was a boy behind you."

"A little guy," added Steven. "We're wondering if you recognized him."

"Lemme think," said Mia. "Like in the morning, right? I was going down the sidewalk . . ."

"Late morning," agreed Steven.

"OK, yeah. Right. I did pass this one kid . . . I don't know his name, but I met his older sister. She started at my school in spring. They're from Somalia."

"Or Ethiopia, maybe?"

"Yeah! Ethiopia, sorry. The dad's a scientist. He teaches at USC, I think."

"OK. But it was her brother? For sure?"

"I didn't talk to him, but . . . wait. It's not about the hate mail, is it? Shelley told me. That is *so* effed up."

"Well . . ."

Saul glanced at Steven.

"But don't say anything, OK? We don't want to accuse anyone. We saw him on the camera. We just wanted to know."

"We could be wrong."

"We probably are."

Mia made a lip-zipping motion.

Bette Midler stood up on his hind legs, paws against the gate. Tail wagging frantically.

"He wants to go in," said Steven.

Mia stuck an arm over the top of the gate and patted him on the head.

"Trust me, Bette Midler. You wouldn't like the swords."

When they regained the sidewalk—Bette Midler twisting around on the leash and whining—Steven said they should keep walking. Check out the house of the scientist.

"It's the Craftsman with the Lexus that's always parked in front," said Saul. "Not the Craftsman with blue trim. But *should* we? Isn't it stalking?"

"Don't be ridiculous. We're just out walking Bette Midler. As innocent as the trees."

So they did. It was irrational, but Saul felt nervous.

He was the rule follower; Steven was the rebel. As a teen Saul had been a mathlete, perfectly content to spend weekends doing his father's taxes, while Steven hung out with taggers and pyro-maniacs. Smoking pot and burning down the backyard sheds of local racists. One had turned out to be an actual Klansman, with a garage full of white hoods hanging on hooks.

Steven had never been caught. And never regretted it, either.

Drawing near, they saw someone in the front yard.

"It's the wife," whispered Steven.

She was gardening. A slim, elegant figure.

Bette Midler chose that very moment to do his business. On a purple head of ornamental cabbage.

The two of them hovered, Steven holding the baggie, as the wife straightened up from her pruning.

She put down her shears and shaded her face with a hand to look over.

"So sorry," called Steven. "We'll clean it up, of course."

"Oh! Not a problem," she said.

Started to walk toward them.

"I'm Saul," he said. "And this is Steven."

"Of course! My name is Amala. We met at the ice cream social."

Cheekbones to die for. Smiling.

"Your dog's so cute," she said. "I always wanted a dog. But my husband's allergic."

"Allergies," nodded Saul. "I know how bad they can be. I get hay fever."

"What's his name?"

"Bette Midler."

She laughed. "We watched *Beaches*! What a tearjerker. But I have to admit, I cried."

"Who didn't," said Steven. "You don't want to, and you're embarrassed, but it's mandatory."

He handed the leash to Saul and bent down to pick up the stool. It was a very loose one. Revolting. He had a bit of trouble.

"Hey, please, don't even worry," said Amaya kindly. "You know what? After you go, I'll get the hose."

"That's above and beyond," said Saul. "Thank you!"

"Disgusting," said Steven. "We owe you one."

"Not at all. It's nothing. I promise."

Steven did his best to tie off the baggie. But it was a horror show.

"So nice to meet you, again," said Saul as they retreated. "And sorry for the mess."

"I got it on my fingers," said Steven.

He held the baggie at arm's length as they walked home.

"Thanks very much, Bette Midler," said Steven. "Whose idea was it to get a dog, anyway?"

"Yours. Definitely yours."

"So *Beaches*, huh?"

"I think of him more as a *Down and Out in Beverly Hills* type. Or *Ruthless People*."

"She looks like a supermodel and she's out there cleaning dog diarrhea. That woman is a jewel."

What they should do, said Steven, washing his hands in the powder room, was figure out a way to meet the kid. Out in the open. By accident, seemingly. But with his mother present. Not say anything obvious, just shoot him a knowing look or two.

After that, Steven was betting, he would stop.

And if he didn't?

Steven shrugged.

"I guess we get rid of the mailbox," he said. "Buy one that hangs right beside the front door."

"But the carrier'd have to walk up to the house."

"It's still Janeane. I bet she'd do it, if we tell her why."

"Janeane's good people."

"It'd be better than stressing out Amala."

"Anything would be better."

"She's a queen among women."

What was it with this kid? Jessie, Saul's niece, was around the same age—maybe a couple of years older. She was so pro-gay it was suffocating, even to him. Never shut up about it. Her peer group punished each other for *not* being gay or gender queer. It was sign of rank uncoolness to be both straight and cis. When she came over with her parents she'd mock them openly for their heterosexual, gender-normative identity and try to rope Saul in.

Awkward. His sister had always been great. As young adults they'd bonded over which men were hot and which weren't. Hell, Joan had gone to Pride with him since he came out in the nineties, swathed in rainbow paraphernalia from head to toe. He'd appreciated the gesture but wished she'd tone it down. Rainbows were so tacky.

"I mean, at least you were *born*," he'd said to Jessie once at dinner. "So *that's* a silver lining."

She'd rolled her eyes and said his generation had Stockholm syndrome. Self-hating.

"I don't think that's what Stockholm syndrome means," said Joan.

"It's when you love your oppressor," Jessie had retorted.

"Well," Steven had said, "your parents have never oppressed *me*. Except for the time when they gave us those concert tickets to James Taylor. Now, *that* was cruel and unusual punishment."

"It was unfortunate," offered Saul's brother-in-law. "A weed thing. I admit."

"I said I liked *Lili* Taylor. We were talking about *movies*."

"I still don't know how I made that translation," said Joan, shaking her head.

"I blame the Purple Kush," said Steven. "Anyway, Jess, it had a happy ending. We sold the tickets and made out like bandits."

The hater kid was bucking the trend. In his demographic.

"Like, why all the anger? From this little boy?" he asked Steven in the kitchen.

It was fajita night.

"Maybe he's in denial," said Steven, slicing an avocado. "Afraid of his own urges."

"Don't you want to use the avocado slicer?"

"The knife works fine. Kicking it old-school, here."

"Why did you buy the slicer? If you were never going to use it?"

"I *didn't* buy it. It was a stocking stuffer. *You* bought it."

"Oh."

"Anyway. The kid's probably going through something. A phase. I say we wait it out."

"I just want to *know*."

"But maybe you can't. That's kind of the deal. With anger. And with hate. Right? I mean, where *does* the hate come from? Fear? But why? What *is* there to fear, honestly? About someone else's romance?"

"A mystery. I guess."

"We never know where it comes from. Only where it goes."

MIXOLOGIST

When he started at the big-box store he'd admitted to a coworker that he'd graduated from Stanford. Rookie mistake.

He'd been trying to keep up the banter. That was it. As a flex, it would have been a dismal failure. Who bragged about Stanford when they were working as a stocker at a big-box store?

If you were *about* to go to Stanford, maybe. If you'd already gone, not so much.

Stu was short and shifty-eyed and had a chip on his shoulder—a drywall taper by trade but maybe not getting much work, since he had to put in a lot of hours at the loading docks. He'd asked where Nick had been working before and Nick said, Oh, I was in school. Stu asked where, and it didn't occur to him to lie.

From then on his moniker was Mr. Stanford. He'd be bent over shelving fruit snacks and Stu would saunter by and say, "Why, good *morning*, Mr. Stanford. How are you *feeling* today?"

He said the same line over and over, like it was comic gold. And spread it to the other guys.

Talking to each other, they left out the Mr.

"Where's Stanford? There's a pallet of cage-frees in the middle of the aisle! Nearly got smashed by a fat fuck in a motor cart."

"Reading *Moby-Dick* on the john, maybe."

Or, if there was a trivial problem that could be solved in under a minute, Stu might say, "Put Stanford on it. I hear his brain is *huge*."

"And wrinkled," another guy might say. "The wrinkled brains are better than the smooth ones. I saw it on YouTube."

"Big brain means small sac," said Doug, who was basically Stu's sidekick. "I'm pretty sure."

It didn't get old for them. He worked there for nine months and after the first two days never got called by his actual name. And it wasn't the kind of good-natured ribbing that led to acceptance.

He tried out various responses: first he owned it, self-deprecating and sarcastic. The other guys hated their jobs and talked racist shit about the managers—"Fu crashed his car, did you hear that? On Sepulveda." "He's a slant, man. They can't drive for shit"—so he'd tried to roll over and take himself down. Like, "Fancy school, yeah, but here I am, right?" But that didn't make a dent. They were MAGA and could tell he wasn't in the club. Instead of giving him a pass, Stu leaned in and slowly leveled a pointing finger at his nose. Then said, "You're not a Jew, are you?" "He looks Jewy," said Doug. "*Jews* go to Stanford," said Stu. "It's all Jew. All the time."

He'd thought about reporting them. But it was everyone. Literally.

Next he'd switched to combative jocularity, trying to match their crassness. "So where did *you* go to school, Stu? Up your mother's ass?" Stu cackled at that one, slapping his thigh. "Up her ass and out the other side, dude. It was a *ride*."

Finally he settled on bored impatience.

In retrospect, changing it up must have looked like weakness. He should have done bored impatience from the start.

Bartending felt like a refuge. Some of the customers liked him and left him generous tips—the clientele was mostly older gay men. There was no razzing at the bar. You didn't make fun of the guy you were depending on to pour your drink stiff.

Also, they didn't know about Stanford. He wouldn't make that misstep again.

He'd never talked about the stocking job to his friends from school. Hadn't concealed it and hadn't needed to. It was their own lives they wanted to talk about when they called him. Most of them were in tech or had startups—they'd gone to recruitment fairs while he was buried in *The Silmarillion*.

Standing behind the bar made for decent anecdotes, at least. He could tell them about sloppy drunks and one-sided hookup attempts. Although there weren't that many. The place was sedate and dimly lit, with imitation Tiffany lamps and stained glass. A tasteful gastropub.

Two of his regulars, a couple that sat at the counter, liked to talk about their dog's diet. They always came in at five and were gone by seven—a Brit and a tall, distinguished-looking African with an accent who wore colorful dashikis.

"Sweet potato is good for her digestion," said the Englishman once, "mixed in with lamb, but the blueberries you like to toss her . . . I don't know."

The African said blueberries were excellent for dogs. As they were for people. Because of the antioxidants.

Bella was a Boston terrier, they told Nick. She turned up her nose at strawberries and raspberries but wolfed down blueberries.

"She knows what's good for her," said the African.

"Not true," said the Englishman. "That little bitch gobbles up cat litter whenever she can find it."

"Where does she get cat litter?"

"A friend's house. No one you know. She only eats the blueberries because they're coming from *you*. And she craves your affection. Since you rarely bother to pet her."

"Come on. I pet her whenever I remember to take my Zyrtec," the African protested.

All this was said quietly—they never raised their voices.

One sleazy guy always wore a T-shirt that had Joe Biden's face on it with devil horns. The T-shirt wasn't popular with his fellow patrons. He kept trying the same pickup line on younger men, something about Little Miss Sunshine, which he'd trot out when a young guy came up to the bar to order. On one occasion it almost worked.

But then the young man saw the T-shirt and took his drink off to a two-top.

The day drinkers made an aimless passage through the afternoons. Complained about chronic back pain and medical bills as they nursed drink after drink. And barely tipped. The trick to good tips was landing the evening shifts. But at first he only got those shifts when someone called in sick.

Chaya liked to sit at the bar and talk to him, but when she did his tips shrank noticeably.

"I could pretend I'm your sister," she suggested.

It wouldn't work, he told her. She didn't look like his sister, for one thing. Their skin wasn't the same color.

"One of us could be adopted," she pressed.

Truth was, he couldn't flirt if Chaya was there. She cramped his style.

Then the main barkeep, Rigoberto, quit to move to the Bay Area and focus on his modeling. He showed Nick pictures on his phone. They involved bondage outfits. Whips and chains and black masks.

Rigoberto said it was a stepping-stone. His manager promised.

Nick had his doubts—Rigoberto was buff, but his face looked like one of those cartoon bulldogs with an overbite—but it was fine by him: he got the evening shifts.

His parents were not impressed.

"What *I'd* like to see," said his dad, "is a career path. Something that harnesses your *potential.*"

"Something, you know, white collar?" said his mother.

"That's classist," said Nick.

"Precisely," said his dad. "This is America, son. We're supposed to be upwardly mobile. Not downward plummeting."

"But also," said his mother, "it has better benefits. We can only keep you on our health insurance till you turn twenty-six."

The discreet couple were anxious. Their dog was at the vet's. Had to have surgery. The Englishman held his drink shakily while the African comforted him. "She's in good hands," he said softly. "The best. You being so anxious won't help her."

"But I have to go home alone."

"I know. And I'm sorry for that, Ken."

"When *you* go home, there'll be people around you."

It was a slow night, only a handful of patrons, and Nick found himself mulling over the exchange. They seemed joined at the hip, but one had a separate family.

Kenneth was the name on the Englishman's credit card, but when the African paid he used cash. So Nick didn't know his name.

Pouring out the next round, he noticed that only the African wore a wedding ring.

Uh-oh.

Still, he could be wrong. His mother had lost her wedding ring for years, till his father found it while he was unclogging the drain of the kitchen sink. "A treasure in the P-trap!" he'd announced, holding it up to the light.

They weren't letting up on the career subject.

"Don't you want to use your *mind*?" said his mother.

He knew why she was saying it. But what would his mind *do* if he used it? He wasn't going to be a surgeon. He wasn't going to replace the failing hearts of poor children. Didn't have the personality, much less the training. All he'd ever wanted to do was tell stories.

But stories seemed more and more useless. The sound of fiddling while Rome burned.

His mother had come in to sit on his bed and talk to him. Closed the door behind her. An indication it was serious.

She held a slim book.

"It's so neat in here. You've really upped your game. On the room-cleaning."

"Thank you."

Having to keep the bar area neat had gotten him into the habit. He realized he thought better when there was less mess.

"Listen, Nicky. Do you think you may be depressed?"

"I don't know," he said. "I'm just, I guess, wondering what it's for. All the striving."

"That sounds *exactly* like depression."

"I'm not exactly sad, though."

"Depression feels more like apathy, I read. Hopelessness. A flat, defeated feeling."

He thought about it. He didn't want her to be disappointed in him. He'd love to give her something, in fact. Something great.

But he had nothing to give.

"What if that feeling is real? Like, a feeling that reflects reality?"

"I mean," she ventured, "it could still be depression."

"But if it's rational, then it's not just an *affect*. Or a *pathology*."

"But maybe it's the kind of thing where, once you're on the other side of it, you'll be like—what was I *doing*?"

"I guess."

"So . . . there's this book. It's short. But very intelligent. I thought it might be good for you to read."

She handed it over. *Darkness Visible* was the title.

"OK."

"And . . . would you talk to someone? Just as a favor? To your father and me?"

"Sure. Hell. I'll talk to anyone."

He could give her that, at least.

Kenneth came in by himself on a Tuesday. Early—before six.

He carried a large picnic basket, the kind that was woven and had two flaps on top that opened from the middle. He might have been returning from a country picnic. Or watching sculling on the Thames. A tennis game at Wimbledon.

He was wearing a navy blazer with beige chinos. One night he'd worn an ascot. But he'd carried it off.

He set the basket on the stool beside him.

"Can I get you the usual?" Nick asked.

The usual was a Manhattan. He didn't make them for anyone else.

"No, nothing yet. Thank you. I'm waiting."

"Sure. Take your time."

Kenneth just sat there, staring down at his hands on the bar, so Nick moved off a bit, giving him space. Cut up some limes and lemons. Served another regular, at the bar's far end, who was making a list.

That customer was always making lists. One time he'd left a list on a cocktail napkin, which Nick had glanced at as he tidied up. It turned out to be songs, under the heading Death Cab for Cutie. *I Will Follow You into the Dark. I Dreamt We Spoke Again.*

Out of the corner of his eye, he saw Kenneth fold his hands together, then point up the forefingers, touching.

Here is the church and here is the steeple. Open the doors, here are the people.

But he didn't open the doors. So there were no people.

His face was motionless. He looked down so steadily that Nick couldn't see his eyes.

Idly, he began to scratch at something on the counter.

"Sorry," said Nick. "Did I miss a spot? Lemme get that."

He hefted his rag, clean and dry. Kenneth withdrew his hands to the edge as Nick dabbed at the speck.

It was only a nick in the wood—didn't come off—but still. Ritual duly performed.

"I met him in Eritrea," murmured Kenneth. "Abraham."

First time he'd heard the husband's given name.

Someone's husband, anyway.

Kenneth had a fond, distracted expression.

"Eritrea," repeated Nick. "East Africa, right? Near Ethiopia? And Sudan?"

Global Human Geography. Sophomore year.

"I was posted there. By Her Majesty's Diplomatic Service."

"Oh. Queen Elizabeth?"

"Indeed. That was the Majesty."

"It's hard to get in. To be a diplomat. Isn't it?"

"Fairly competitive, yes."

"Far away! So how did you end up in LA?"

"I resigned, eventually. When he got tenure here. So I could live near him."

"Seems like a sacrifice."

"It was. But I thought it would be worth it."

Nick said nothing. He'd learned that from Rigoberto: when you saw muddy waters, don't wade in. Further the conversation, Rigoberto had advised, punt it along if you have time, but don't be intrusive.

Kenneth was a study. Stiff upper lip—restrained. But you could see the love on his face.

"Anyway," he said. Pulling back into his shell like a turtle. "I suppose I'll have that drink now, please."

Nick handed over the Manhattan as the list maker flagged him down for a refill on his Jim Beam. Asked him if he was a Gemini.

"No," said Nick.

"A Scorpio, then?"

Also no.

"OK," said the list maker. "Third time lucky. Sagittarius!"

"Sorry," said Nick. "Uh, Taurus. I think."

The list maker was crestfallen. Also, seemed disbelieving.

"I *never* would have said Taurus."

Abraham had come in. Stood just inside the door, hesitating.

As he made his way toward the bar Kenneth turned his head and rose from his seat.

Nick moved slowly into earshot, escaping the talk of star signs. Which was high on his own list. Of bar subjects to be avoided.

". . . not one of our *days*," Abraham said. Annoyed, maybe. He was there under duress, it seemed. "I had to leave his soccer game at the halftime break. And he was already angry at me. He's so *angry*, lately. It's almost as if he *knows*. Could he have seen one of our emails? Or a text?"

Standing beside his picnic basket, Kenneth looked like he wanted to say something, then kept his mouth shut. With one hand, opened a flap on the basket.

Abraham peered in. And jerked his head back.

"Oh *no*."

Kenneth started weeping loudly. In ragged sobs. Abraham looked stricken, but after a few moments moved to put his arms around him. Awkward. Patting mechanically and gazing in Nick's direction. But not really seeing him.

His eyes were watering too, but he was self-conscious.

The list maker was straight-up staring. And a few people at tables. The place wasn't busy yet: Kenneth crying was the whole scene.

The two of them were caught in a spotlight. Nick felt protective.

In the corner was a dark booth, so hidden that customers liked to fondle each other back there.

He lifted the bar flap and went through, touched a light hand to Kenneth's back as he sobbed. Gently guided him into the booth. With Abraham following.

"My basket," said Kenneth. "I need Bella!"

"I'll get it for you," said Nick. "You just sit down. It's more private over here."

The basket was heavy. Carefully lifting it, he felt no shifting of weight. And knew for certain the dog wasn't alive.

He poured a beer for Abraham, who didn't drink hard liquor, and carried it over with the Manhattan. The basket was open on Kenneth's lap, and Abraham sat beside him, looking down at it. Both the flaps had been removed.

Inside, swaddled in blankets like a baby, lay Bella.

A little black-and-white face.

He turned away quickly. Leaving them to their grief.

Dogs weren't allowed inside. Some guys tried to smuggle them in, Rigoberto had told him. "They act like the dogs have a total right to be there. You gotta be firm. No dogs. And, at the bar, no kids."

But a dead dog didn't pose much of a threat. Except, maybe, in the eyes of the Health Department.

He wasn't closing—he was supposed to meet Chaya for dinner—and when he handed off the register to Evan, the other night tender, Kenneth was sitting alone in the booth. Abraham had gotten up to go to the bathroom. So Nick went over to say goodbye.

The cover was back on the basket.

"He was all I had," said Kenneth. Almost a whisper. "But I don't have him."

Over food-truck Mexican, sitting across from him at a rickety table in a gravel lot, Chaya droned on about LARPing.

He'd been done with it for weeks, but she wouldn't let it rest.

It was how they'd gotten together. Without it, as a couple, she didn't know who they *were*.

Looking at her after she said that, he felt far away. There was a tinge of regret, but mainly distance. Like she was at the far end of a telescope.

Another person who wanted him to be someone he wasn't.

Chaya's dad was rich, a self-made man with a fleet of food trucks not unlike this one. Divorced, and she was an only child, so she was spoiled. He'd given her a Tesla for her eighteenth birthday. The model where the doors opened upward like wings.

When she let him drive it, he felt like the pilot of a rocket ship. It was all white inside.

2001: A Space Odyssey.

It was nice to ride around in, though. In a capsule like that, the dirty streets disappeared. With their panhandlers and flapping tents of homeless encampments and gray film of exhaustion.

You might lift off. Up into the universe.

"We could just be us," he said.

"But then what do we *do*?"

"Something else?"

"But Nicky. I'm still *into* it."

"You can LARP without me. You don't need a Son of Ragnar. You're a High Priestess."

There was no going back. He saw it, now, as pitiful.

He was so far down another road that when he looked back, that version of him was a tiny figure in silhouette.

At the end of the telescope. With her.

But his pity wouldn't hurt her too much. She still had the Tesla.

The discreet couple stopped coming in after Bella. Some afternoons, as the cocktail hour approached, he found himself waiting for them.

But they never showed up.

Maybe they went to a different place. Embarrassed and starting fresh. He searched for Kenneth on social when the bar wasn't busy. Using the full name from his credit card.

But Kenneth was too old for social. Or too refined. All he found were a few links to diplomatic news—minor items from years ago. A reception at an embassy. A quote about food aid.

At the bar, people entered and exited at will. You couldn't track them down or stay in touch. You were a temporary fixture for them, like the counter.

He told his sister about it. How the couple had vanished. How he wished he could know the path their lives were on. Have them sit at the bar again and see how they were.

She was off at Berkeley, but they FaceTimed a couple nights a week. Did edibles and set their phones up on their desks.

She'd been his self-appointed antagonist, when she lived at home, but not anymore. They'd gotten into the habit of talking when she started asking him about how to do course selection and balance the credit requirements. Their parents didn't know the drill, and her advisor was useless.

So now she felt closer. Though farther away.

And more open. Less sure of herself, but in a good way. She was paying attention. In high school she'd been like a blank wall of Popular Girl. With some Mean Girl thrown in. She'd done what she wanted and thought she was the bomb.

But now she worried about actual bombs. She was taking a class on nuclear proliferation.

"With Putin and China and North Korea posturing, we're building up our arsenal again," she told him. "It's the biggest buildout since the sixties. They're making new plutonium pits at Los Alamos. So the ICBMs in all those creepy silos buried in the middle of the country will get a makeover."

She also worried about her boyfriend. Technically, her husband, but Nick thought of him as a serious boyfriend. Just with an extra piece of paper.

She couldn't have a real husband at her age. No matter what she called it.

And who knew? That piece of paper might stop him from getting deported, one day.

Luis worked all the time, she said, and never went with her to parties. If she was late finishing a paper or tried to skip a class because of a headache, he'd guilt her into knuckling down. Gentle but firm. Don't you know how lucky you are? he'd say.

Sometimes she felt like he was her father. She'd left her old father behind in LA, but it turned out she'd brought a new one with her.

"I can see how it feels like that," said Nick. "But he's not wrong."

Liza approved of his move away from LARPing. Strongly.

She liked to rib him about it. But the ribbing wasn't sharp.

"Bruh. You're finally growing up," she said.

"And fuck you too," he retorted.

He talked to her, in the swimming warmth of the weed, about how he didn't want what he used to want.

How he barely knew *how* to want. Anymore.

For himself, anyway.

What he wanted was for the world to stay. But it was going away. All of it leaving: animals, plants, forests, the polar ice.

While people told stories. And ran around building their résumés.

Wanting to look like winners. Beneath the falling sky.

GERONTOLOGIST

One set of grandparents had died before she was even born. The other lived in Michigan and sent Christmas cards with preprinted messages like Goodwill to Men. They were the kind of Christians that didn't want to hang out with you if you weren't the same as them.

They couldn't *stand* her mother. Blamed her for taking their son away. To godless Los Angeles, her mother said. Her mother had been a godless woman. In a godless city.

After he died they'd never come to visit. Most people would have been curious about their grandchildren, her mother said, but not them. The last time the grandparents had seen them was at his funeral. When Mia was three. And Shelley was eight.

So she'd never known many elderly people. Except her neighbor Miss Caroline. Plus a few teachers and librarians. But they weren't *old* old, since they still had jobs. Whenever she'd spotted old folks, like, roaming in the wild, her eyes had passed right over them.

Maybe, she figured now, it was because their faces didn't

catch the light so simply. Their wrinkles and folds complicated the surface.

You were always looking for beauty when you looked at other people. Is she pretty? you'd think. Then yes or no or maybe. All right or not so bad or wow, he's hot. Every time you saw a new face, your first impulse was judging it.

It was automatic. It wasn't your only data point, but it was one. You barely noticed you were doing it.

Maybe you did it less, as you grew up, but you still did it.

Or maybe there was an even worse reason she hadn't noticed the elders—maybe they'd just seemed spent. If a person was old she used to see them as a waste of space, almost.

It was like, Sure, you can keep on existing, but I'm not personally interested. Because your life has already happened.

The more she hung out at Twelve Oaks, the more she studied old faces. It wasn't that the wrinkles disappeared. Though they did seem to fade a bit. Instead they showed a history of expressions. Their personalities were carried by skin. You could tell who'd smiled a lot—they had more crow's-feet at the ends of their eyes.

Often the elders weren't in a hurry. And yeah, sometimes it was because they didn't have a destination. Sometimes they had nowhere they had to be. Or if they did, it was just mealtime or a nap. So it was relaxing, hanging out with them. Some weren't so bright and never had been, while others used to write books or command armies.

But what they had in common was, they were coasting.

She thought of it like skiing, which she'd only done a few times but liked. In skiing you took a lift to the top of the mountain. Getting on the lift was rushed and busy, handling your poles and managing your skis. If it was crowded, you had to make sure they didn't get tangled up with other poles and skis. Then you waited while it carried you to the top. Maybe you made some conversation with the skiers beside you.

And then you went down. There might be obstacles, and maybe you had to concentrate a little and manage your body. But at a certain point, you took on speed. It was like you floated. Gliding past the trees. You could look around at the hills and forest and the drifts of snow.

Eventually it would end—you recognized that. But meanwhile you were suspended. In the freedom of the air.

The elders were in the coasting part. So they could see a lot. There were still obstacles, but they were flying down. Instead of struggling to get up.

Sometimes when she hung out with her same-age friends after a day at Twelve Oaks she'd get bored of what they talked about— clothes they wanted and shows they'd seen. Or people they knew on social who were racist or transphobic. She'd wish she was back with the elders, then. The elders were tired of separateness. They might want to be together or to be alone. But either way, not argue about categories or privilege.

Meshugas, Lucy called it. All that meshugas. People denouncing each other for the tiny details of what they said.

"It reminds me of Stalin," she said. "And the Stasi."

She clucked her tongue and shook her head.

Lucy had met Stalin once, she claimed. At a parade when she was little. He never knew she was Jewish, she said, because she had yellow-blond hair. In ringlets. My mother bleached it, she told Mia. And her own, too. Some Jews have blond hair naturally. But no one around where we lived.

"Stalin was very short, you know," Lucy said. "Five foot six. Like Napoleon."

After she taught the elders to work their phones and tablets— and sometimes had to reteach them—she'd found other tasks she could perform. Things the staff didn't have time for.

Lucy liked to put on fashion shows and make Mia rate her outfits on a scale from 1 to 10. Or Mr. Hammond, who was in a wheelchair, had her rearrange the Hummel statuettes that used to be his mother's.

He'd be all, "Wait, can you put Hello World beside Little Girl with Basket? What do you think? No—I don't like. Try beside Boy with a Red Bunny. There! That's better."

Mrs. Ovedo had gotten upset because she couldn't pluck her eyebrows anymore—couldn't see them without her glasses on. But *with* her glasses on, which were big and round, she couldn't reach them with her tweezers. Once she'd poked her eyeball with the tweezers and burst some blood vessels.

Her thin, arched eyebrows were her pride and joy. So she told Mia how she liked them and Mia plucked them for her. Twice a week.

Sometimes it was more serious. The staff were supposed to be handling the residents' meds but didn't always stay on top of it. Some residents had medication lockers and some, in Independent Living, didn't. And the staff nurses were mostly nice, but busy and stressed. So Mia went around looking at medication sheets and comparing them to the pills in the day-by-day trays. M, T, W, TH, F, SA, SU. When they'd been put in wrong, which wasn't unusual since some of the pills looked similar to others, she'd rearrange them.

She worried about that. When her gap year was over and she went off to school, who would check for them? Who would make sure?

She took pictures of the pill trays for the elders, once she knew they were right, and then pictures of the orange vials they came from. Drew big, bold arrows to the compartments, with the number of pills that had to go in each. Printed the pill guides out and hung them in bathrooms. Of course, the meds got adjusted now and then, and then she'd have to do it over again.

Mr. Hammond's meds got adjusted a lot. He'd been in the Air Force, he told her. But he hadn't dropped bombs, he said. He did troop transport.

"In a war?" she asked.

"Yes, dear. That's what the troops were for. The Korean Conflict. 'Fifty-two and 'fifty-three."

"That makes you really old, I guess."

"I'm ninety-two."

"I never would have known," she said. "You don't look a day over eighty-eight."

"Ha ha," said Mr. Hammond. "Cute *and* a comedian."

Another guy, who everyone just called Bob, had Alzheimer's and on bad days thought she was his first wife. He'd say things that were inappropriate. Like, "I don't think you should show so much of your body, Ellie. That skirt is too short for you." Or, "That shirt is much too tight. That shirt is for a baby!"

Actually he was dead-on: it was a onesie she'd found in a thrift store that said Top Gun. She'd cut off the bottom part with the snaps.

He tried to hug her from the side when she was near him and even tried to kiss her on the cheek.

"Now Bob, I'm not Ellie, remember?" she reminded him. "I'm Mia. You know me. I'm your great-granddaughter's age!"

Then he'd get confused in a different way and feel ashamed. And when he felt ashamed he'd try to give her his belongings.

"Take the rubber ficus," he said once. "It doesn't get enough light there anyway. But it's a good plant. It's such a good plant."

He reached out a hand, patting the leaves sadly.

Or, "Here, would you like an electric toothbrush? It's a brand-new Phillips. Top of the line. Still sealed up in the box. You see?"

His first wife had died when she was in her twenties. Mia found that out from a photo album he showed her.

"You look like her," he said on a lucid day.

The photos were blurry, but maybe there *was* a resemblance. It wasn't that much of a stretch.

"She's been gone a long time, hasn't she," said Mia.

"Seems like forever sometimes. Other times it feels like yesterday. Time . . . collapses," said Bob.

He held out his hands in the air and moved them together.

He'd had a second wife too. For forty years, before she also died. But it was only the first one he talked about.

Mia felt sorry for the second wife.

Bob said people had invented time. That it was all at once and everywhere. But minds weren't able to grasp that, so they had to divide it into sections.

He lifted up his day-by-day pill tray. "Like this," he said. "A grand illusion."

"How can it be all an illusion? I mean, it *matters* which day it is. Plus there's you. And there's me."

She meant young and old. That their bodies went in one direction and finally fell apart.

Bob nodded. "It's physics, apparently."

"But what about biology?"

"Physicists don't have time for biology. It's too alive for them."

Before he retired he'd been a chemical engineer. She admitted she wasn't sure what a chemical engineer did.

He'd made potions, he said, like a witch with a cauldron.

"A bad witch?" asked Mia. "Or a good one?"

Bob smiled sadly. "I think I was a bad witch, in the end. I wanted to be a good witch. And make things grow better. Like corn and sunflowers. But it turned out I was making poison. Don't let it happen to you, sweetie. Don't see it all as some big game. And spend your life making poison."

On his lucid days he was one of her favorites. On the other days he was a hassle. She let him hug her, but she had to draw the line at cheek-kissing. It wasn't his fault, but his lips were slobbery.

Lucy had a thing with Bob, and also with some of the other old men. She was all about romance.

"It isn't the sex," she said to Mia. "It's being seen. If you want to know the truth, the sex isn't so great, these days. For me. From my end. Even with the blue pill."

"TMI, Lucy," Mia would say.

"It's the affection. And the attention. With sex, you're the star of the show."

But Lucy's romance with Bob added to his befuddlement. She'd only "lock the door" with him on lucid days. On the other days, there'd be no door-locking. And then, when he didn't think Mia was Ellie, he might think she was Lucy. Which was worse, because he was handsy with fake Lucy.

When he thought she was Ellie he was tame, considering that Ellie had been his wife. But when he thought she was Lucy he'd try to grab her butt and ask her for some "afternoon delight."

"No delight, Bob," she'd say, and swat his hand away. "I'm gonna go now. I have to play Uno with Mrs. Ovedo."

"Play Uno" meant pluck eyebrows. Mrs. Ovedo didn't like her to mention she was doing it.

"It's our little secret," she said.

She wanted to seem put together. All by herself.

A nurse who wasn't one of the nice ones came in on a day when Bob was being handsy. She got way harsh as soon as she noticed it.

"You shouldn't be dealing with this," she said to Mia, right in front of him.

Then she turned to Bob and told him in a mean voice that he was out of line. Acting like a pedophile. She even used the word: *pedophile*.

He looked as if he'd been slapped. His eyes watered instantly.

"No, hey, it's really OK, Bob," said Mia.

She went to comfort him, pulling a tissue from the box on his bedside table.

"Don't baby him. You'll just encourage it!" said Nurse Ratched.

In English Lit they'd had to watch *One Flew Over the Cuckoo's Nest*. Which had a mean nurse in it.

"But it's not *like* that with Bob," Mia said. "He won't *remember*. It's how he feels right now. That's all there *is*."

Then Nurse Ratched stalked out of the room. She must have gone to talk to someone in Admin. Because a lady Mia had never met before stopped her in the lobby as she was leaving.

Her nametag said Lauren. Guest Services Director.

"You've been a help around here," she said. "Many of our seniors are fond of you. But you're eighteen years old. You're simply not qualified to make care interventions."

"Oh! It wasn't an *intervention*, though," said Mia. Scared of the lady, suddenly. "I'm just his friend."

"Of course. But you're not family," said the lady.

"He doesn't *have* a family. They left him here six years ago and moved to Uruguay."

"Be that as it may. I've had a complaint from staff. And there are liability issues. I was willing to overlook them, at first, but I can't do that anymore. Since a complaint was made. I'm afraid you'll need to stop coming in."

Mia stared at her. Could she do that?

"But I help them out. A few really depend on me."

"I'm sorry. It's the way it has to be."

Driving home, she felt her hands slip on the steering wheel. Sweating so much she had to pull over.

She thought of all the pills getting in the wrong compartments. Mrs. Ovedo and Bob crying.

"What *is* it?" asked her mother in the kitchen. She came and took Mia's hands. "What happened?"

She couldn't speak. Afraid she was going to lose it.

She closed her eyes and counted to ten. Then told.

Her mother got tight-lipped.

When she was mad, her lips went in a straight line. Her face turned steely.

"Make me a list," she said. "Of the residents you're close to. With their cell numbers and room numbers. And write down how you help each of them."

"What are you going to do?"

"Don't worry. Go out and have some fun. You haven't been going out much. Isn't Liza back in town from Berkeley? For the long weekend?"

"Yeah. I haven't seen her yet."

"Hang out with Liza. And say hi for me. But first, make me the list."

It got long—thirteen people. Beside Mrs. Ovedo's name, under the heading Tasks, she typed *Personal Grooming.* Beside Bob's name, because she helped him shave, she typed that again. And then again for Lucy because Mia touched up her roots. Every three weeks.

The list made her seem like a stylist.

She wasn't sure about including the pill-organizing. It could count as a care intervention. Even though she was just fixing what had been done wrong. One time she'd stopped Lucy from taking a triple dose of her antidepressant. Another time, reading a chart to check the dosages, she'd discovered Mr. Hammond had been given Paxil instead of the Plavix he needed.

She'd googled it—Plavix prevented blood clots. And therefore strokes.

She told her mother.

"Write it down," said her mom. "It could be useful. If I have to get threatening."

Liza was in her brother's room when Mia got to their house. He sat in his desk chair and she lounged on his bed, laughing hysterically. "No way, no way," she repeated.

When she got up to hug Mia, she was still laughing.

"What's so funny?"

"Should I tell her?"

"Oh, man," said Nick. "I don't know. I feel bad for him."

"She won't say anything. Right, Mia?"

"I could use a laugh right now. So yeah. My lips are sealed."

They looked at each other and burst into gales again.

"Close the door, though," added Nick. She did. And sat down on the bed next to Liza.

"So here's the caper," said Liza. "If you pinkie swear."

They hooked pinkies. A ritual since first grade.

"Before I left for school, I was sitting at the desktop in the TV room. You know, that old piece of shit we only use for, like, grocery list spreadsheets. My dad was watching one of his cycling races on TV. I opened up a browser and started typing. But it autofilled this porn site. I figured it was Nick's deal, so I was all, Dad, holy shit! Nick's been watching porn! And he was all, Oh *my*. I'll have a man-to-man with him."

"Embarrassing!" said Mia.

"So I mentioned it to Nick just now. And it turns out it wasn't *him*."

"I mean, I've watched porn, now and then," said Nick. "It's happened. I freely admit it."

"We don't need to know, Nick," said Liza.

"But not on the family computer! In the TV room? That thing is like, ten years old. It takes five seconds to load a basic page. I'd have to be a moron."

"*Nick*," said Liza, "you can't say *moron*."

"Stupid. Can I say stupid?"

"My dad was all, Don't mention this to anyone. So I didn't."

"Till now."

"Yeah, well—I didn't pinkie swear. So."

"Right," nodded Mia. "The promise was meaningless."

"Exactly. So it was *him*! It was my *dad*. And the kicker is, it was this weird fetish porn where young guys . . ."

She screwed up her face in a grimace.

"Say it," said Nick, grinning. "You're almost there."

". . . young guys were doing it with grandmas. Like, old ladies."

"Oh, TMI!" squealed Mia.

At first it sounded shocking. But then she thought of Lucy.

"Well, but. I mean. How old's your *dad*? Like fifty-five?"

"My mom is *not* an old lady," said Liza. "Except for the Zumba classes."

"Good thing Luis didn't come down with you," said Nick. "Don't tell him. It'll make our whole family look like pervs."

"How can I *not*? I tell him everything." She turned to Mia. "He has a new job as a paralegal. In training. He couldn't get time off."

"Just don't," said Nick. "Dad practically worships him."

Liza was undecided.

"People should be allowed to have their secrets," ventured Mia. "Sometimes it's kinder if you let them."

"Dad tried to pin it on you, Nick," said Liza. "You should be out for revenge."

Nick cocked his head. "I'm not," he said. "Let sleeping dogs lie. That's what I say. He really admires Luis. So let him keep his dignity. In front of him."

Liza still looked torn. Mia changed the subject.

"Hey, how's Chaya?" she asked Nick.

He shrugged. "I think she broke up with me."

"You *think*?" said Liza. "Don't you, like, *know*?"

"It wasn't a hundred percent. There was a gray area. Like I was on probation. But I don't need to be. I'm good with the breakup."

"She was pissed because he wouldn't do LARPing anymore."

"Oh," said Mia. "That's too bad. I liked her."

"They wanted different things," said Liza, mock-sighing. "In her case, to be a High Priestess for all time."

"Your backyard was my last LARP," said Nick to Mia. "I had a revelation. Not an epiphany where the light shines down. Just like, What the hell am I *doing* here?"

"You kind of had that look. Standing there staring at the others. Like you were outside it."

"You want a weed gummy?" he asked her. Held out a baggie.

"Sure. Thanks."

Maybe it was the gummy, but when she got home and saw her mother at the kitchen island, DMing with Lucy—Lucy was a night owl—it looked like her mother had a halo.

A glowing light around her head. Like the Virgin Mary.

She used to resent how her mom got so involved. She was one of those tiger mothers, if she perceived an injustice.

And she always perceived an injustice.

At school, when Mia was tapped for violating the dress code and just wanted to go home and change and come back, her mother had rushed in raging from the parking lot, straight to the principal's office. With Mia standing right beside her, trying to sink into the floor, she said the dress code was sexist. And she'd be damned if her daughter was going to be body-shamed using taxpayers' money. Aka, hers.

"Don't make me get serious with this," she said.

The principal said they would let it go *this* time.

Or also, when Mia had been into soccer in ninth and tenth grades, and the ref made a bad call that wasn't in her favor, she was one of those parents who yelled at him in front of everyone.

But now how she felt, watching her mother text with Lucy, was taken care of.

She couldn't bear never to go back to Twelve Oaks. And leave the elders on their own.

Up in her room, she lay on her bed imagining she was a resident there herself. She was *so old* . . .

She was sad to be old. And not OK pretty anymore. She missed herself, young. Scenes of her lost youth passed before her like a movie.

But she was also wise.

She was all about oneness, now. Not division.

Tomorrow she and Liza were going to the beach. Just to walk and maybe watch the surfers.

She would stare out at the water when they got there. The ocean was a great oneness.

Above her hung a mobile she'd dug out of a box, from when she was small and in a crib, and put back up again.

"Why did you stick it away in a box?" she'd asked her mother.

"You told me to. That was during your pink princess phase. The solar system was irrelevant."

It had the planets circling the sun, lit from within. Jupiter was her favorite, with its stripes of yellow and red.

She pictured herself as an elder. The orbits of others were ringing out around her, colorful worlds traveling in ovals, again and again and again. Into eternity.

She might have satellites.

Or she might be a satellite herself.

What was the difference? They were all revolving.

Liza insisted they drop in on her brother at his bartending job. "I want to see him in his *element*," she said.

It was a restaurant, so they wouldn't get carded at the door.

"But it's mostly for gay men, isn't it?" asked Mia.

"Sure, but it's slow in the afternoons. We won't stay long. Just one drink."

"OK. But only if you don't try to make him serve us," said Mia. "It would stress him out. And he could lose his job."

Liza could be a terror. When she was in her stubborn mode.

"Fine. Mocktails only."

It was a dark place but fancy, not divey. With stained glass in the windows, blocks of brown and orange. They made it feel peaceful. Like a sanctuary.

Behind the bar Nick looked handsome. She hadn't thought of him that way before. Like with the elders, almost. She'd known him since always and never noticed it. He'd just been Liza's big brother.

They sat down on stools.

"Wow, Nick," said Liza. "Lord of all you survey."

"I like to think so. But I don't survey a lot. Do I."

"Say it."

"Say—?"

"You know. Your lines."

"Uh . . . what can I get for you ladies?"

"Ew, gross!" said Liza. "I hate being a lady!"

"Don't worry. You're not one."

He opened them a couple of nonalcoholic beers and went to serve a couple at a table.

"I'm still bothered by the image of your dad," admitted Mia. "Watching that porn."

"Oh my God!" said Liza. "I forgot to tell you. It wasn't him after all."

"It wasn't?"

"No. So like, I told Luis. I had to. I tell him everything."

"And?"

"He laughed. And told me it was *his* browser history. He didn't even hesitate. It was research for some free speech case he was studying. Where this porn site was the issue."

"Oh, good!" said Mia. "That's totally a relief. Now I can look at your dad again. And see him as a father figure."

"Me too!"

A sketchy-looking guy with a ponytail came in, and even though there was no one else at the counter and all the stools were free, he picked one right beside them.

Didn't know they had skeeves at gay bars, typed Liza on Mia's phone.

His grubby T-shirt had an old-man devil face on it. He ordered a pint when Nick got back behind the bar.

"Hey Nick! You know that white guy who used to come in with the black one?"

"You're going to need to be more specific. We have more than one African American patron."

"Come on. You know. He used to come in with the guy that wore those print shirts. With the, like, colored embroidery."

Suddenly Nick was paying attention. He set down the pint.

"Kenneth?"

"Yeah, right. That's it. I heard he"—and he made a throat-cutting gesture. Drawing a finger across his neck.

"*What?*" asked Nick.

His face had gone strange.

"He offed himself," said the skeevy guy.

"But . . . you didn't even remember his name! How can you *know* that?"

"I knew his name. I just forgot it for a second. I heard it on the gayvine."

"No," said Nick. "I don't believe it."

"Believe it, dude," said the skeeve. "Hanged himself by the neck. Till he was dead. Channeled Kate Spade, I guess."

Nick looked at him. Hard.

"You know what, Dylan? These girls are my family. We need a little privacy. So do me a favor, just this once, and take your drink to a table. Would you?"

The guy made a grunt of annoyance. But he slid off the stool, sloshing beer from his glass as he went.

Nick wiped it.

"Nice smackdown," said Liza.

"*Ass*hole," he said under his breath.

"But did you know the man he meant?"

Nick was clutching the bar rag too hard, turning his fingers white. He kept on wiping even when there was no more spilled beer.

Mia put her hand out and caught his wrist.

"It's OK, Nick," she said. "Hey. Take a deep breath."

"I like him," he said. "He's British. He used to be a diplomat. His little dog died. Bella."

"You don't have to talk about it now," said Mia.

"And it might not even be true," said Liza. "Like you said."

Nick threw his rag in the sink and turned to the cash register.

She got a call from the Lauren lady saying she could come back. But please, be deferential to the nurses. And she'd have to sign something.

Mia wanted to retort that she was always deferential. Except to Nurse Ratched.

"We did a petition," Lucy told her proudly. "Your mother's idea. Twenty of us signed it."

They hugged.

Nick asked to come with her one day. After Liza went back up to school.

He was curious, he said.

When she introduced him to Mrs. Ovedo, he got a whole speech about how Mia was an angel. An angel of mercy.

Mrs. Ovedo believed in angels and saints. She kept an altar to the Virgin of Guadalupe opposite her bed. It had a painting of the Virgin in an arched wooden frame, wearing her blue shawl with white stars sprinkled on it. Plus, at her feet on a little ledge, fake flowers and small wooden animals.

There used to be votive candles, too, but open flames weren't allowed so they'd made her get rid of them. Mia had brought in some twinkly lights and helped her string them up around the Virgin. Mrs. Ovedo liked to lie in bed and press the remote that controlled them. She could make them flash or burn steadily.

"After I'm gone," she said to Mia, "I don't want you to be sad. You don't need to be. OK? Because you will know that the saints and the angels came to carry me home."

When she took Nick to meet Lucy, Lucy exclaimed: "What a handsome boyfriend!"

"No," said Mia, "he's my best friend's brother."

"Oh, I *see*," said Lucy, but she winked at Nick cringingly.

"It's not the worst idea," said Nick as they were leaving.

"What?"

"Me being your boyfriend."

"Get out," said Mia.

Her face felt warm.

"I mean, you're an *angel*, they tell me."

"*So* not," she said. "I like it here, is all."

As he drove her back to her house it was a little quiet. After what he'd said.

"So," she said. "Listen, did it turn out to be true? About the man at your work?"

He leaned forward over the steering wheel. Adjusted his position in the seat.

"Forget it," she added. "It's none of my business."

"No, I can . . . he, yes. He did kill himself, I guess. At least, he died. There was an obituary. It didn't say how, but I don't think he was sick."

"Nick, I'm sorry."

They stopped at a red light.

"It's just . . . I'm depressed myself. I don't have suicidal ideation. But I can understand."

"You can?"

"I think he just felt alone."

"Yeah?"

"His boyfriend was a bit younger than him. A professor. But the boyfriend had a whole other family. A wife and a kid."

"That's sad."

"They'd been together for years. The two men. Just during the daytime, a couple of times a week. But I guess he was still hoping."

"That the other guy would leave them?"

"But he didn't want to wreck the family. So he didn't force the issue. And then, one day, their dog died. Bella. The Englishman's dog, mostly. He was really attached to her. And maybe it was then that he decided the other guy was never going to leave. And be with him."

Someone honked behind them.

"Oh, shit," said Nick.

He gunned it.

PASTORALIST

Damsels in distress, was how he described them to the beer boys. To himself, he said sheep. He was a shepherd. Gathering in the strays.

A sheep was fleecy and warm. Often plump. Plump was ideal, in sheep. Up to a point, of course: pleasantly plump, not morbidly obese. A fatted sheep was properly humble. Whereas a slender sheep had attitude. What a fatted sheep needed was a fleecing: to give up the weight of all that wool. And what he offered was to take it.

They posted flattering pictures. Selfies taken with the chin jutting out so you couldn't see the flabby neck beneath. Or from above, like on a pillow, so the flesh fell back from the bones.

But he was an expert. He could read the angles.

Once he secured a meet-up, he did his Flash routine. His personal Patrick Bateman. Grooming, lifting, getting pumped. Taking his pills and supplements. So when he presented to the sheep, he was psyched.

He couldn't come on too strong, though. A sheep was wary

when she was separated from the flock. Afraid of wolves—a natural impulse. He had to roll over, showing he was more like a pet than a predator. Expose a tender underbelly.

That was one of the best parts of the four F's. The Flash routine, when he made himself look and feel his best, was followed by the Feint routine. Flash, then Feint.

He'd had to think hard, when he started out, about what his feint should be. What was believable, coming from a guy who looked like him. Why would he ever be insecure? Given his advantage?

He tried different approaches. But the one that worked best was the simplest: past trauma. A wound had been inflicted and left him hurting. Secretly haunted and unable to inhabit his exceptional good looks with the expected confidence.

Typically he went with the loss of a beloved sibling. From an accident or a long, drawn-out illness. He didn't dwell on it. Excessive sympathy would be a buzzkill. Just made a fleeting mention.

The third F was Feasibility, when he assessed his chances and brought it in. And the fourth was obvious.

Occasionally the fourth was less obvious: Failure. It didn't happen often. But did it happen? Yes. Some sheep weren't ready to be fleeced.

They used to have 4-H clubs, when he was a kid. His Mima had always wanted him to join one. Because she'd belonged, back in the 1950s. He forgot what it stood for. Something with Home or Hearth, maybe. Or Heart.

It involved farming, anyway. Tending to barnyard animals. Like sheep. So his personal club was 4-F.

Some of the fleecings were one-night stands. The apps he used weren't Tinder, since the sheep he preferred weren't really the Tinder breed, so they weren't supposed to be one night.

They were supposed to be "love" matches. Same as with pets. "Find Sparky his Forever Home," it said, on dog-adoption websites.

The apps he used were like that, but for people.

If the fourth F was disappointing, he'd stop at one night. Done and done.

The best lasted for weeks. He'd had a sheep he strung along for five months, once, till she got irritating.

His club should be 5-F, honestly. With the last F being Fade. For fade away. The fade wasn't as good as the other four F's, but closure was a crucial step. He let them down easy so they could limp back off into the pasture, shorn. In places, bald and patchy.

But 5-F wasn't a play on 4-H anymore. So the last F was more of a PS.

If they pissed him off, though, he *didn't* let them down easy. If a sheep turned insulting, during the fifth F, he was forced to do the same. He'd shake his head at how dumb a sheep was, reading her messages.

It's cowardly, you ghosting me like this, one of them had baaed. *And cowards are weak. Even if they have bulging pecs.*

That sheep had thought she was bringing out the big guns. But being a sheep, she couldn't handle guns at all. No opposable thumbs. Didn't know a Ruger from a Glock.

He did, on the other hand. A regular Stephen Paddock. Minus the mass murder.

Depending on how the sex had been, or if the sheep was tech-savvy and had the potential to retaliate, he'd either do a full final feint or, in a small minority of cases, blast them away with an AR-15.

In text form, of course.

The full final feint, his standard go-to, would be: *I'm so sorry to disappoint you, I'm having a personal crisis. My mother died and I can't see anyone. I'm so so sorry. I'm just a total mess right now. I hope you'll forgive me.*

Partly true, in a sense. Though his mother had died in '96.

And it repeated the first feint, but that was OK. A repetition of trauma made it doubly tragic.

An AR-15 volley would look like, *I didn't want to say this. I wanted to protect your feelings. But you're just too fat for me.*

Most of the sheep stopped bleating after that one.

A few, before he learned how to manage his profiles, had posted warnings. But then he learned work-arounds and used different emails and cell numbers. He knew how to fade, these days.

In a way he was doing them a favor. What doesn't kill you makes you stronger.

If a sheep went on a diet after he faded, good. Healthier sheep.

If a sheep was wiser from then on, and maybe put her guard up more, well, that was all good too. Survival of the fittest.

He'd kid around with the beer boys, sometimes, watching a game and shooting the shit, about the newest damsels. Most of the boys were married or had a steady girlfriend, but he didn't get together with couples. Didn't enjoy family hangouts, either. The wives asked prying questions and came as a package deal, with kids. Who whined and got all their attention.

The beer boys liked hearing his stories. Gave them a break from their boring lives. One woman had so many cats in her apartment it felt like an animal shelter. Smelled of urine. "Oh, *man*," Malone would say, "that is *raw*." Or, one liked to call him Dirty Daddy. Another prayed the rosary before they did it.

Sometimes the beer boys would exchange shifty glances, during a story, and he'd dial it back. Slap on a joke at the end.

He didn't take sheep back to his place. Not a single sheep had ever seen where he lived. In a pinch, he'd spring for a hotel.

He kept a list of all of them, an inventory, and for two years running, before COVID, the list was over a hundred.

Then lockdown hit and he was shit outta luck. Still found some willing sheep, but he had to troll MAGA websites and anti-masking forums. Pickings were slim.

And honestly, the sheep were lower quality. With liberal women out of the mix, the median was older, uglier, and whiter. It almost made him want to switch party affiliation.

At a retro diner the beer boys liked to eat at for tradition—Wiff and Malone used to go there when they were young—he was telling a juicy tale one evening when a frizzy-haired girl steered alongside their booth and clapped her hands over Wiff's eyes.

Startled, Wiff knocked over his half-full drink, spilling watery soda onto his burger plate. Then the guys tried to soak it up with thin paper napkins as the woman apologized. And in the middle of the shitshow Wiff stood up to hug her.

His favorite niece! He hadn't seen her in two months! Why aren't you coming to the barbecues, sweetiepie? We miss you!

"This is Collette," he said. "We call her Letty. Since she was a kid."

That was when Les got a gut flutter.

Letty was a sheep from last year. With an asterisk beside her name because she'd been a hard exit: the AR-15.

He remembered because he hadn't planned to use the hard

exit. She hadn't earned it. No pissed-off accusations, just like, Where are you? Hey you! You've disappeared!

She should have been a full final feint, for sure. He hadn't minded her. Almost, a couple of times, felt a tug of affection.

Whenever he felt a tug like that, he knew it was time to cut bait. Or get sucked down into the dark waters.

A shepherd had to plant his feet on solid ground.

After he sent the text, then scrolled back through a couple of hers, he realized he'd meant the hard exit for his Tuesday. Not Thursday.

Sometimes an AR-15 strafe went wide.

And damn. In the vastness of the LA metro area, what were the chances?

She was nodding and greeting. Wiff said they could make room. "Shove over, folks."

And then her eyes settled on Les.

Double-take. The smile wiped off her face.

"No way," she said. "Uncle Wiff. You *know* this guy?"

"What guy?" said Wiff.

"Him," and she pointed.

Bad manners to point, Mima used to say.

"Les? A buddy from my old gym. When we lived in Silver Lake. You two *know* each other?"

"Les?" she said. "No! Wiffy! He's the guy with the . . . he's the one who texted. And broke up with me."

Wiff looked back and forth between them.

Les sat forward, shaking his head and pretending to look more closely at her face. "Honestly, I think you're making a mistake," he said. Keeping it light. "I really don't know you. I'm bad with names. But I'm decent at faces."

She leaned over to Wiff, cupping her hand around her mouth and whispering in his ear.

When she pulled back again her eyes were watering.

"Shit," said Wiff. "Are you sure?"

She nodded. Dabbed at her eyes. Pale, quavery. "Yes."

"What's happening?" asked Malone. "Is there a problem?"

"Of *course* I'm sure! His face. And voice. His body. Everything! It's just *him*!"

"This is, uh," said Wiff. "Wow. This is above my pay grade. Les?"

He was wedged between Malone and the wall. Trapped.

"Listen," he said, tilting his head to one side. "I don't get what's going on. But I'm not someone she knows—I never met her till tonight."

"That's just a *lie*," said Letty. And started sniveling.

Wiff put a hand on her back. Pat pat.

"Uh, so . . ." said Malone. "Listen, Les. Either way, you should probably take off. We can sort it out later."

Les wore a sad face. Injured.

But shit yeah. Secretly relieved. To get the hell out of Dodge.

The beer boys slid along the bench and stood up. Les scooted over. Awkward, but he kept his sad face on. Baffled and sad.

He reached for his jacket, hanging on a hook between the booths, and she shrank back. As if he was planning to hit her.

Bullshit. That was Rule Number 1: Never hit a sheep. He never had and never would. Sheep were for shearing, not beating on. It was catch-and-release.

He wanted to tell the guys that. In case her shrinking back was making them doubt it.

But couldn't. His hands were tied.

"He's the *worst person* I *ever met*," she said to all of them, loudly and trembling.

Les shook his head and raised his hands again. One holding the jacket. But kind of Christ-like, now that he thought of it.

Another good shepherd. Crucified by the Romans.

I am the good shepherd; I know my sheep and my sheep know me.

Mima used to quote it.

He got a text from Malone. *Wiff says no contact,* it said. *Going forward. This is me telling you. Sorry, man. We always tried to cut you slack. But this thing seals the deal. Upside is, she's not going to press charges.*

Press charges? What the hell? For what? An insult?

Wiff was practically a man-sheep—the kind they cut the balls off. Even his name: William Ford was the real one. He got away with a moniker like Wiff because it came from his frat-boy days. And he was blond and rich. A descendant of Henry Ford, was the rumor, but he wouldn't confirm it.

He was the softest of the beer boys. And the richest.

Lifting in front of the full-length in his bedroom, he knew he didn't need them. OK as a group, but in single combat they couldn't have competed.

Malone was a tough guy next to Wiff—a cop turned security guard—but had a flabby stomach. No core at all. He'd let himself go after the hearing. Excessive use of force. The union had been behind him all the way, he said, and luckily the so-called victim wasn't black, just some white-trash tweaker in Altadena, so it didn't make the news. Still, the job was soured for him and he quit.

Wiff had no gainful employment. Just family money and a cute airhead wife he bankrolled. Who talked about chi and arranged flowers.

And the two younger guys, Stu and Doug, were hangers-on—Malone's nephew and his pal. A drywall taper and a roofer who got stoned a lot. And worked at some loading dock between construction jobs.

The trades, Les always called them.

There was a guy at the office who kept trying to pin him down for a drink after work. Thin and stooped with an Adam's apple that stuck out. He hadn't heard any of Les's stories yet. But at a company picnic, when a bunch of them stripped down to their shorts to slosh out a waterslide, he'd gaped at Les's six-pack.

Not a fag, though. Married to a woman. And sharp—their highest earner.

Time to change things up. Find a new set.

Six years now, he'd known Malone and Wiff.

But a shepherd was a wanderer. Had to be.

Still, he had to hand it to Letty. She'd lost a ton of weight.

A success story, in fact. She should be grateful.

Classic sheep. Didn't know what was good for them.

The coworker, Phil, had a tight group of friends who played Dungeons & Dragons. Been playing it since they were teens.

"Naw, man, I never played," he said when Phil asked him. "I'll be straight with you, I always thought it was for nerds."

Phil shrugged that off. "You should come by one time. We don't accept a lot of new people. The last player joined in, I wanna say, 2016. But I mean, you can check it out. Have a drink and take it in."

For a while he hesitated. It had a whiff of desperation, showing up at a dweebfest like that.

But the guys he lifted with at the gym were off limits. As a peanut gallery. You didn't shit where you ate.

He felt Phil out. What did the D&D crew do?

One was a coder, but heavy-duty, Phil said. Worked for SpaceX. One was a hedge fund guy, another a VP at a 3D-printing outfit. One had designed an app involving classic cars. And had some other startup before that. Cleaned up at the IPO. The car app was just a pet project.

Huh. Maybe he was the one to watch. Tech entrepreneurs were the nerd alphas. Plus, classic cars. Boss.

He told Phil he would go with him. Just once, he said. See how the other half lived.

That being the nerd half.

So they drove over to the tech dude's place after work and a beer. Swank property. Spotlights in the vegetation. Inside it was gleaming and new. And so spacious it barely made sense. Like the job of a house was to capture maximum air.

He thought of Mima. Oh *my*, she would have said, nodding and smiling at the host. What a *palacio*!

It was the kind of home she'd been paid to clean. He wouldn't have wanted to bring her there—she would have acted humble and tried to help dish up the food—but he would have liked her to see it. If she was still around. See it without being seen.

Phil led him into the kitchen. Whole marble deal. Italian, he said. Then a word like Calcutta. Or something.

There was a wife, but she was never home for D&D.

"Ironclad rule," said the host. "The D&D games are her girls' nights out."

She'd gone to Georgetown, international relations, and had a lot of friends from Russia and the UAE. A few Saudis.

Good good, thought Les.

"You want a daiquiri?" asked Phil.

"A *daiquiri*?"

Didn't compute.

"We rotate cocktails," Phil explained. "According to the occasion. So like, for St. Patty's Day it might be an Irish shot."

"Right now it's Women's History Month," said the host. "So we thought, What do women drink? Hey, maybe daiquiris."

Jesus H. Christ.

"Uh, sure. Why not. I'll take a daiquiri."

He drained the thing in five minutes. It tasted like dessert. But they were nursing theirs. Turned out they didn't typically have a second drink. Because they didn't want to "drive impaired."

One drink. Well, holy fuck.

There were high-end appetizers, at least: trays of finger food with dabs on them. Crab puffs. Puree on flimsy crackers. Pâté, the host called it. And orange fish eggs. "Salmon roe."

So he loaded up on those. While sitting at a vast table in the dining room. It was made of a single immense slab. Shellacked and thick. No planks. Someone had felled a redwood for that thing.

He remembered a giant lumberjack. Paul Bunyan. A towering statue he'd seen driving through a forest up north. With Mima when he was little.

They started playing. Said nebbish words like *wizard* and *Verily!* in fruity voices. *He's chaotic neutral, so what did you expect?* Monsters were mentioned, such as orcs. Mind flayers. They rolled their many-sided dice. Someone checked something in a book.

Talk talk talk talk, using a code. Chaotic good. Chaotic evil.

Phil turned to him, now and then, helpfully trying to explain. "So there's a circle, in terms of character, with chaos and law on opposite sides. And then good and evil. Neutral's in between."

He nodded and glanced around, wishing he had another stupid daiquiri. On shelves there were vintage toys. Probably fetch a mint on eBay.

He never thought of that trip up north, usually. Paul Bunyan with his blue ox. But here was this massive sequoia in some nerd's house. Plates of crab puffs on it. Dice in different shapes and colors.

What had it cost? Ten grand? Thirty?

He moved his hands across the wood. Felt the grain beneath his fingertips.

He should go see that statue again. And the big trees around it.

". . . you getting any of this, Les?" asked Phil.

"Oh," he said, coming back. "No, just admiring the table."

"My wife found it," said the host. "A Sotheby's estate sale. Something to do with Orson Welles, I think. But I could be wrong."

"Rosebud!" said Phil.

"Rosebud," echoed the others.

No clue what they meant. Was that a D&D thing?

He didn't want to overthink it. But a phrase came into his head: *Out of your league, buddy.*

A kid in junior high had said it to him once. About a girl he'd been eyeing.

After the phrase occurred to him, he started to get antsy.

It was hard to tell under the loose clothing, but he didn't figure any of them had tone or bulk. And the faces were mediocre. Two of them wore glasses. One had a gray goatee, another male-pattern baldness. One was Indian or maybe Pakistani—

his accent sounded like the convenience-store clerk in *The Simpsons*. Abu Dhabi. Full head of glossy hair and a decent shoulder span, but Les detected a slight paunch. Reminded him of Malone's.

Malone, he thought for a second. Almost homesick.

Abu Dhabi was playing the role of a gnome. A gnome with a low charisma score, said Phil, who had to roll the dice to see if he could hook up with a buxom tavern wench.

No, was the answer. They all laughed.

Still, he felt nervous. Didn't get what they were saying. Even when it wasn't about the game. Too many names and references. Like they were all holding a dictionary no one had given him.

He'd had a few sheep like that. With them, he'd change the subject. Bring it back around to what he knew. Familiar territory.

But he couldn't do that here. It was an ocean. Where the waves rolled in and in.

Dark waters.

He had to get away. Back to the pastures. Soft and green.

"Les! You've been so quiet!" said the host.

"He's the strong silent type," said Phil.

"Sorry," said Les. "I guess—I'm feeling a little sick. Queasy."

"Did you eat the crab puffs?" asked the Indian. "Shit, man. Do you have a shellfish allergy?"

"Oh. Huh. Was that crab?" said Les.

He'd heard the host say so. But he could brazen it out.

"Oh, wow. Sorry. I thought I said so," said the host. He scraped back his chair. "You don't go into anaphylaxis, do you? We have some EpiPens."

"Nothing like that," said Les. "Just nausea, is what it is."

"Come on. I'll show you to a bathroom."

Les followed him. Obedient.

"Take your time," said the host, leaving him there. "I know how it can be."

The bathroom was bigger than Les's living room.

But why? Did they hold parties in the bathroom? Debutante balls? Those quintillions?

Stayed in there for a while. Took his shirt off, flexed, and posed. *This* is who you are. A pick-me-up. Then dropped the pose and looked straight ahead. Like for a mug shot.

I'll have to press charges against you, said a hot woman cop. In a porn scenario. She pressed her tits against him. For being so goddamn *built*.

He thought about jerking off, but afterward he'd be low energy.

Why did they talk like that? In code?

Showing off. Nerds had to pose differently. That was all. Long words and redwood tables.

Compensation. Oldest trick in the book.

He didn't want to go back out, but he had to.

Listen, he coached himself. All problems had a solution. And that solution was attitude. He'd go back in on a stream of confidence. Be it, be it, be it. Affirm. Invisible momentum. A rush that propelled you.

But where was the rush? He waited.

One lousy drink.

Too bad he couldn't go in without a shirt. Then the reason for his confidence would be obvious. If he could walk around without a shirt forever, he would. Instead, he had to hide his light under a bushel. An old expression of Mima's.

Don't hide your light under a bushel, dear, she used to say. When he slacked off in school.

He had an idea. It was out there. It was bold. But maybe he could do it! Pull it off!

The tech boys thought he was sick to his stomach. Side note: never. He had a kickass gut microbiome. A probiotics regimen.

But people who were sick threw up.

Should he do it? Hell. What did he have to lose?

He ran his shirt under the faucet, then hung it on the shower-head. Grabbed a hand towel and slung it over one shoulder.

When he walked back in, they turned and stared at him. He wore a shamed expression.

Stood under a hanging light, a few feet back from the table. In all his glory.

"Man, this is so embarrassing," he said. "I just met you guys! But I had to, uh, I kind of had to rinse off my shirt. You know?"

"Oh, shit," said Phil. "Gnarly."

But they were staring. At the figure he cut.

Trapezius, delts and pecs. The rectus abdominus. The transverse intersections. The linea alba. The obliques.

He would have liked to raise his arms, so they could see the lats, but didn't have an excuse.

Staring. And marveling.

"So sorry," he said. "I was just wondering . . . It's hanging up right now, in the bathroom. I used the liquid hand soap. Scrubbed it down. So it's pretty clean. But maybe if you have a dryer? I could toss it in?"

"Uh, yeah," said the host.

"Sorry to interrupt the game."

"Sure, no," said the host, shaking his head and then nodding. Scraped his chair back again. "It's not a problem. Meanwhile, I can get you one of mine to wear."

"Ha ha," said the Abu Dhabi gnome. "Don't think it's going to fit. Man, sorry, but I gotta say it. You are *ripped*."

Murmurs of agreement.

"Oh?" said Les. He gave a quick glance down, dismissive and modest. "Oh! Well, thanks."

In the laundry room, the host was eager to please. They had three washers and three dryers. For when we entertain, said the host. Company functions. Table linens and shit. To help out the caterers and maids. They should rewash the shirt, right? Just to be sure.

He tossed it in a machine. All by itself.

Once the machine was going, he took Les through the master into a massive walk-in. "Maybe one of these? Whatever works," he said.

Les accepted a brand-new white T-shirt from a package in brown paper. The T-shirt package had a silky ribbon on it.

Fit tight as a glove. Made him look like a sculpture. Though he was careful not to check the mirror. Had to be cool.

When the two of them got back to the table, the tech guys seemed subdued. They took up their game again. But now they were trying to include him. Asking about his allergic reaction. How was he doing?

Fine, he said. Much better. In fact, he said, he could use another daiquiri.

Abu Dhabi got up and fixed him one. "You came in Phil's car, right? Plus, not to be too graphic, but you kind of got it out of your system."

Whir-whir, went the Vitamix.

The daiquiris would come rolling in now. If he requested them. Like the ocean.

The waves were turning clear.

"Hey. Les. Listen. You ever do any personal training?" asked the gray goatee. "Like, as a trainer?"

"Not, you know, for *money*," said Les. "But I mean, I could give you some tips. If you like."

"I have a weight room here," said the host. "Never really used it. Ha ha. Obviously."

"Well . . . huh. I'm busy Saturdays, but Sundays are free."

The gray goatee was chomping at the bit. "*This* Sunday? Let's do it!"

He'd brought them to heel. Gambled and won.

It wasn't about strutting. You had to use humility.

The second F, he realized. The feint! But with a new target.

Phil might be the highest earner, back at the office, but here he was the lowest by far, Les figured out as they were driving home. Low man on the totem pole.

Abu Dhabi had a Mercedes Roadster and the SpaceX coder had a Model S. Probably got it at a staff discount.

Phil, on the other hand, drove a small Lexus hybrid. A hatchback. He actually bragged that it had a Prius engine.

"Fifty-two miles per gallon," he said proudly.

The car was practically a vagina.

But man. These guys were tenderloin: the prime cut.

With steers like them in the feedlot, he'd barely need the sheep.

CULTIST

The talent had common features, Marnie said, like racehorses or dog breeds. Their physical traits were well known—oversized heads, eyes, and lips, since these features were babyish and telegenic—but they also had psychological commonalities.

Most of their psyches didn't veer far off a predetermined mean: say, the difference between a Maltese and a shih tzu. Breed standards meant their personalities and biographical arcs were fairly predictable.

It was a given, for instance, that the younger they were when they got famous, the more neurotic they'd grow up to be. Child-star egos got stroked and groomed instead of crushed, like the egos of normal kids, by the stark realities of middle-school torment.

She'd been a PhD candidate but dropped out of grad school. "ABD," she told Shelley. "All But Dissertation. The ivory tower's far behind me now. Just a low-rent neighborhood in the rear-view mirror."

Young talent had a pre-Copernican view of the universe, she claimed. A Ptolemaic cosmology.

"They see themselves as the center of the universe for *years* longer than normies do. The home planet, fixed at the center of all being. With the sun rotating around it. Lighting it up and shedding warmth."

So each career setback gave them an existential shock—a deeply destabilizing glimpse of a sun that might not be circling around them after all. Instead they turned into planets far out in lonely space. Bathed in shadow, away from the burning core.

Gender was also a determinant. Male child actors were typically at higher risk for substance-abuse disorders and a stunted narcissism that might develop into a persecution complex. While the females suffered less from delusions of grandeur—the moderating influence of sexism, Marnie figured—but more from depression. Men used substances and got antisocial; women turned anxious and depressed.

"Men flail around hitting out at the available targets," said Marnie. "And women aim their harming impulses inward."

With the talent, regular gender differences were grossly magnified. Women were almost guaranteed an eating disorder. Due to the scrutiny of crowds. Her educated guess was 85 percent. You *did* see female addicts and male anorexics, of course—your Lindsay Lohans and Christian Bales—but those were exceptions that proved the rule.

Some clients she dismissed as variations on a theme, but others she worshipped. A select few, she told Shelley in a hushed voice, were unearthly. The glow around them lifted them up and separated them from mere mortals. As though they were *beatified*. Their charisma was a bristling field—almost an emanation of divinity.

"Star quality?" asked Shelley.

"But *more*," said Marnie.

Her body language changed when those celebrities came near: she kept a fixed smile on her face and rarely turned away. Like a courtier who walked backward out of the throne room after an audience with the emperor.

But the bristling field wasn't coming from the talent at all, Shelley would have argued if Marnie had been willing to listen. It came from their handlers and entourages and agency staff. The assistants, the lawyers, accountants, receptionists. And the agents. Like Marnie.

Marnie was a true believer, even with her reductive categories and statistics, where Shelley was outside the programming. The field was tangible, yes: you couldn't deny its existence once you'd been in a room. But it was produced by excitement and anxiety, which peaked, in the presence of the famous, into a pheromonal flop sweat laced with adrenaline.

Because livelihoods were at stake. Careers could be shattered on a whim.

The actors themselves did not glow. Or when they did, it was the result of daily personal training. The right drugs, well dispensed and calibrated. Excellent makeup, at times. Plus dresses or shirts that cost five grand a pop. Minimum.

The trick was not to get caught in the field. It wasn't easy: anxiety was contagious. And once you were caught, you generated your own field. A sympathetic field. Pulled in by the gravity of other objects.

That was where Shelley relied on a cosmological model herself. You turned into a satellite, if you let yourself get drawn into a planetary orbit. In that position, all you could do was reflect light.

There was no life on the moon.

But it was a delicate balance. When it came to the need for ass-kissing, the clients weren't a monolith.

Some of them were so fragile and rarefied they couldn't have a basic conversation with a normie unless it was laced with pandering compliments. Only when they encountered another famous person, say on a set or at a party, could you glimpse any humility. Then they might bow or genuflect, according to the fame and money hierarchy. Or turn confessional and fake-intimate.

The more mature among them, though, were relieved to talk to someone who didn't reinforce their special status. They were bored and exhausted by praise: it was white noise to them.

You had to know which talent fit which profile, however. And you had to find out fast.

Shelley developed a minor hack for this, though it came with risks. She'd make a small, deliberate error, say in a drink or snack order for a meeting, and assess the response. You could tell a lot about a celebrity from how they treated a minion's mistake—the spectrum of attitude was a tip-off. Hissy fit; cold rejection; casual remark; good-natured acceptance; total indifference/they didn't care or notice.

She couldn't do it regularly or she'd be pegged as incompetent. So she had to pick her moments with care. She usually had a backup ready, the correct order waiting in the wings. Handing around, say, a tray of coffee-related beverages from the Starbucks on the ground floor of the building, she'd give the famous person a latte almost identical to her own. Just, maybe, lacking a sprinkle of cinnamon. If they noticed, she'd swiftly switch out the drinks.

You could score a point with a famous person by happily drinking from the cup already marked with her lipstick/his acne-scar concealer. On one occasion a celebrity, not naming any names but Annette Bening, had been grossed out by this. But even in that case, it got chalked up to standard operating procedure. Who *wouldn't* want those famous germs?

Mostly they never touched their drinks anyway. Once the drinks were served and the gesture made, they ignored them. A ritual offering.

Marnie was successful, sure. But she could be even more so, in Shelley's view, if she lost her religion. So Shelley's tack was to watch her closely. See how she might improve upon the master.

Executives were a tougher brief: data-dependent. Where the data was their histories and personalities, their greenlight ability or lack of it, and their entities' current financial positions. Marnie kept all the intel in her head, an invisible map of the city she navigated out of sheer instinct. Where Shelley had to resort to a hasty GPS. Like when you were driving and grappled with your phone. Trying to bring up a route in the middle of traffic.

She entered the data into a spreadsheet where executives were cross-referenced: their exes and friendships, the grudges they bore, their possible private agendas. In a way they were the opposite of the famous, since their power lay in what you *didn't* know about them.

They were the *éminences grises*, said Marnie, which Shelley had to look up since she didn't speak French. It meant "gray eminences," the powers behind the thrones.

They weren't gray eminences, Shelley thought, but actual royalty. And the talent were pawns, easily sacrificed if they failed to make bank.

But fine. Let Marnie throw around some French.

No piece of information was too small. If Marnie said, about a senior creative exec at A24, "She doesn't eat sushi," it went into the spreadsheet. So did "Oh, him? He's born-again AA. Won't even glance at properties about good-looking alcoholics."

Jake, who was working on his MBA, had a passing interest in celebrity gossip but no respect for her career. To him it was purely social. Qualitative, he said. Mushy. He got off on picoseconds and algorithms. Enjoyed pattern recognition and probability.

He also enjoyed his pit mix, who had behavioral problems.

Jake was rigid in his personal habits. On the spectrum, Shelley suspected.

The dog, on the other hand, had a personality disorder. Psychotic, was her guess. He had to wear a muzzle on walks ever since he bit part of the ear off a miniature schnauzer.

And Jake had to pay the vet bill. Or face litigation.

When she first met Jake she'd thought he was a dream come true. Looked like Tom Cruise if he were younger and taller. Even got mistaken for him at overpriced restaurants. Until the tourists realized Tom Cruise wasn't in his twenties anymore.

She hadn't known about the rigidity until it was too late.

Now her attraction was weakened by his uptightness. If a plate got put on a shelf in the wrong place, or a sharp serrated knife went through the dishwasher, he'd get self-righteous and controlling.

In the apartment, order and hygiene reigned. With antibacterial soap placed in strategic locations. Even before the pandemic.

On the other hand, it didn't bother him at all to leave Geronimo's turds all over the backyard of their rental.

He also wasn't bothered to own a pit bull named Geronimo.

He claimed it was because, as a puppy, the dog had jumped off a boulder when he was taking him for a hike in Fryman. Scared some hikers.

"It was an ambush," he said. "Like the Indians used to do. Or guerrilla warriors."

"You *literally* can't name a dog after a great Native American," she'd told him. "I'm serious. I can't even call him in public. You need to rename him."

"It's a cool name," he said.

"It's not."

"No, but it is."

That was the level of their exchanges.

He started to remind her, after a while, of the talent. Except that he wasn't famous. And never would be. Best-case, he'd end up as a quant at a soulless hedge fund.

Their apartment was in a house with a hippie couple who seemed to run an informal soup kitchen. Transients went in and out of the front door. Sometimes camped on the porch. She and Jake had a separate entrance and rarely had to talk to the hippies or homeless men. The apartment section of the house, as a rental, had been redone with a modern, concrete angularity designed to appeal to guys like Jake.

She felt bad about the dogshit, though, and when it got bad she'd nag at him to pick it up. He'd shrug and say the landlords were slobs and wouldn't even notice.

On rare occasions when he went into the main house—say, to hand over the rent check—he'd come back quickly and douse himself in hand sanitizer.

Eventually she'd have to go around the backyard with a plastic bag and tongs. Cleaning up after a mentally challenged pit bull named for an Indian war hero who died in a white man's prison.

She'd listen to music while she was doing this. And daydream of breaking up.

It was a liberation fantasy. Triumphant, like a makeover montage. But afterward she'd tell herself, Maybe next week. Hey! Good to have something to look forward to.

Jake had other ideas. He'd been asking for months to meet her mother.

"You won't get along," she told him. "She's a painter."

He didn't get artists. The kind of speculation they engaged in, he said, was irrational. An artist said to her- or himself, I'm going to make some random thing and toss it blindly in the direction of the market. Like monkeys hurling their feces at people at the zoo.

"I like monkeys," said Shelley.

"But I don't care what she does for a living," said Jake. "I just think I should meet her. You're my girlfriend!"

In many ways he was borderline stupid.

Good at math, but stupid.

Her mother would see right through him. She'd know Shelley had gotten into it for the sex. And stayed because of inertia.

And her mom already thought she was heartless.

"Mercenary," she'd said once, talking about Shelley's job. "Isn't it a bit *mercenary*?"

Capitalism, she meant.

Shelley had said, "It's the landscape we live in, Mom. You and me both. You think people would commission your portraits in a socialist utopia? At fifty grand a pop?"

"In a socialist utopia," her mother had said, "they wouldn't need to. I could paint them for free. Or in trade."

"Barter the paintings for carrots and toothpaste," said Shelley.

"It'd be a shitload of toothpaste," admitted her mother.

So Shelley kept putting it off.

Till finally she figured, Hell, maybe it'll be the last straw I've been looking for.

When she said she was bringing him over, her mom said: "Oh, let's make it a couples dinner! Mia can bring the guy she's dating."

"What guy?" asked Shelley.

"She hasn't told you yet? It's Nick!"

"Nick, *Liza's* brother? The cosplay dude? He's *my* age!"

"It was LARPing, not cosplay."

"There's a difference?"

"Anyway, he doesn't do it anymore."

"Small mercies. Still, kind of old for her."

Mia was the ditz; Shelley was the serious sister. They'd both gotten A's in high school, but Mia scored a 1380 on her SAT to Shelley's 1520.

But now, thanks to an outreach project Mia was doing with local senior citizens to get out of the house in her gap year, their mother saw *her* as the grounded one. A social campaigner in the making.

Which her mom had always wanted them both to be. Probably to compensate for her own life painting trendy pictures of rock stars and actors.

Jake wore a suit jacket and brought flowers and expensive wine. He was stiff and anxious, going in.

"Don't let her see the sanitizer wipes in your pocket," Shelley hissed at the front door. "She'll think you're OCD."

Which, probably.

Mia and Nick were already there, dutifully setting the table.

Shelley noted the boyfriend contrast: one clean-cut and Tom Cruise, the other a laid-back hipster with shoulder-length hair.

Alpha and beta males, possibly. She'd known Nick slightly back in high school. He'd been a grade below her and always had a girlfriend, played sports, and was sought-after. A teenage role model.

It wasn't obvious which of them would be the alpha. In a dinner-party setting.

She made the introductions in a hurry and poured herself a glass of wine. Jake said No thanks, he'd wait for dinner.

Her mom gave him a quick tour of the ground floor as Shelley tagged along holding her glass. She always did that with first-timers, to make them feel at ease, she said. People liked to know where the bathroom was.

Jake stopped in front of a framed portrait.

A print, but he didn't know the difference.

"Is that one of yours?" he asked her mother.

Her mother laughed, assuming it was a joke.

But then her mother glanced at his face. And realized it hadn't been.

It was van Gogh.

That was the first gaffe. Shelley took a sip of wine and decided to count them.

At the table, waiting to be served, he rearranged his cutlery. The knife had been pointing the wrong way. He was itching to rearrange the other place settings, she could tell.

Luckily, he couldn't reach them.

The knife didn't qualify as a gaffe, though. No one noticed.

Once they were eating, he asked Nick what he did.

"Dread," said Nick. "I live in terrible dread."

"Pardon me?" asked Jake.

He was on good behavior. It was usually just What.

"Oh, you mean to make money," said Nick.

"Uh, yeah," said Jake.

"I bartend. At a gay bar."

"More of a gastropub," added Mia. "The food's delicious."

"Oh," said Jake. "But you don't have to be gay to work there?"

"No. They don't check your sexual preference credentials."

"I went to a gay bar once," said Jake.

Shelley closed her eyes. Oh God I don't believe in. Please deliver me.

Nick waited. Then gave up.

"Oh, sorry. Was that the whole story?"

He didn't say it meanly, more teasing, but Jake wasn't great with humor. Unless it was slapstick. He needed tone indicators. In real life.

He kept eating. Sort of distractedly.

Mia jumped in. Shelley wanted to kiss her.

"I'd *never* gone to one before," she said. "I mean, I'm underage. But also, I thought it'd be rude. Because it's a place for a *community*. So you're like, intruding. But at Nick's restaurant the guys are accepting."

"Mia's like a mascot," said Nick. "The patrons think she's sweet. But don't worry, Ms. B. She doesn't *hang out*."

"I'm not worried," said their mother.

"What about you?" Mia asked Jake. "What's your profession?"

"Getting my MBA. USC."

"Ah, business. And what do you plan on doing with it?" asked her mother.

"Selling himself to the highest bidder," said Shelley. "Right, J?"

"Uh, yeah. Right. Basically."

"So would that be in New York?" asked her mom. "Wall Street?"

He shrugged. Chewed some lasagna and swallowed. "Could be. Not a complete given."

"Are you going to move to New York with him, Shelley?"

Slyly bomb-throwing.

"Hell no," said Shelley. "It's Hollywood all the way. For me."

"Uh, but I have another year after this," said Jake. "To decide."

"Anything could happen!" said Mia brightly.

"The market could collapse," suggested Nick. "Under the weight of its own bullshit."

"Highly unlikely," said Jake.

"Really?" said Nick. "You think?"

"It's not a question of *thinking*," said Jake.

"No?" asked Nick. "Isn't that what speculation is? You know— the definition?"

"Oh. Well, I . . ."

"And the markets are all about the future. Aren't they?"

"One hundred percent," said Jake.

"So, if the future disappears, and the semblance of predictability, so will the structure of the markets."

"I mean . . . how would the future *disappear*?"

Nick set down his glass. Then started laughing.

Jake shot a sidelong glance at Shelley. A look of confusion.

"Sorry," said Nick. "Sorry."

But he started laughing again. A tinge of hysteria, maybe.

Stopped himself. Cleared his throat.

"He means the climate?" said Mia. "Sea level rising? Ice melt and mass extinction? And like, wildfires and storms. The West burning and the East flooded by hurricanes. You know, the chaos. That's probably coming."

"Oh," said Jake. He nodded, accommodating. But condescending. "An increase in stochastic events. Greater disruptions in the supply chain. I get it. Believe me. We model them all the time."

"You *model* them," said Nick. "Cool cool cool cool."

"The models are very sophisticated," said Jake. "You wouldn't believe some of the new variables we're embedding."

"Embedding the new variables," nodded Nick. "For sure."

"But I agree," said Jake. Earnestly. "You're gonna see some wild swings. Down the road."

"Wild swings," repeated Nick. "High market volatility."

"Right!" said Jake. "Medium term. And long."

Nick nodded. Then shook his head. Looking down at his plate.

"The corrections will likely be dramatic," added Jake. "At times."

"The corrections," murmured Nick. "At times, quite dramatic."

There was a silence. Prolonged.

"Well!" said Shelley's mother, putting her hands together. "How about dessert?"

She moved them onto the deck for tiramisu.

Good, thought Shelley. A change of scene.

There her mother asked Jake about his own family. Checking the boxes in the getting-to-know-you routine.

But that road ended in a cul-de-sac. You couldn't draw him out on the subject.

He said they lived in Nebraska and weren't that interesting. "I don't know. Like, a normal family."

"Oh yeah? I'd like to meet one of those," said Nick.

"Maybe they just don't live in *dread*," suggested Shelley's mom. Grinning at him.

"Yeah. They're the lucky ones," said Nick.

He could give as good as he got, Shelley thought.

She *did* have the wrong boyfriend.

"I mean, they go to church," said Jake.

Don't fall into a trap, she was thinking. Stop talking. But before she could interrupt, he kept on going.

"My dad's a Scoutmaster. He coaches Little League."

She met Nick's eyes.

Don't let him say anything about liking young boys, she prayed. Oh God I don't believe in.

He didn't. But she swore she could see the thought bubble.

"*Leave It to Beaver*," he said instead. "All-American."

"Nice to know it's still an option," said her mother.

Driving home, Jake was quiet for a few blocks. She thought of her mother's pitying look after the van Gogh incident and prepared herself to offer comfort. Summoned a halfhearted reassurance and waited to deploy it.

"That went really well," he said. "Don't worry, babe. I liked her."

FUTURIST

Crypto wasn't his bailiwick: Bitcoin bored him, and currency markets in general. The speculators, the hype and the fraud and the good old Ponzi schemes in slick new disguises, paled into banality before the spiritual revelation of AI. The greater mind, the cloud mind, the ethereal—untethered digits of the novel sublime, the streamlined and superhuman nextness of the now.

That one was his. The "superhuman nextness of the now."

He didn't like to get down in the weeds—had no interest in being an academic's academic, lacing his prose with neologisms that would make a lay reader's head spin. He was chasing a grander patrimony. A feeling he'd had, once, with an epic soundtrack in his ears, running on pavement early one chilly summer morning.

He'd been into wearing toe shoes then and felt the nubbly asphalt against his soles. Running past massive container ships in an industrial port, glittering glass towers in the distance.

Hamburg? He wasn't sure. Maybe it had been Stockholm. A trip he'd taken to northern Europe. In the port he'd seen concrete and metal all around. And when he glanced up at the clouds, a dense swoop of black dots that were birds.

What birds? He'd had no idea. Later he'd found a similar sight on YouTube.

Swallows. They formed and re-formed in graceful, morphing shapes in the blink of a human eye. Celestial choreography, said the video caption.

He'd understood it right away. The birds were barely alive. More like fragments of information in the sky.

And then he'd had the feeling. Power. Euphoria. The smooth, hard glint of steel.

Flesh into digits, wings into pixels. Blood and oxygen into will, will into majesty.

When laypeople feared the rise of the machines, the most basic of them still saw robot armies. Like in the space movies. Soldiers of mineral and polymer, overrunning those who had only soft and breathing bodies. They failed to envision the authentic hereafter already vested in their searches and browsers and algos—decentralized knowing, the ghostly form of a universal nervous system that shifted and flowed over the globe like weather or birds. Into the homes, out of the homes. Into the halls of commerce and government.

That was where he came in. An illuminator, for those with lesser powers of sight, of the kingdom to come.

In the base world of bodies, sure, you'd have some cyborg adaptations down the line. Microchipped corgis were a humble gateway. From pets to children, was how it would go. Any day now the privacy paradigm would flip. Security experts already knew it. Safety would beat out autonomy, in the eyes of the helicopter parents. Hands down. Find My iPhone without the iPhone—Foucault's panopticon in action. Asymmetrical surveillance. Inserted neatly into those plump baby arms. As smoothly as the removal of a foreskin at a bris.

Meanwhile the robot makers over at MIT were little boys, playing with their Transformers. Struggling to make their animal-form toys perform the elementary motor functions. Clinging stubbornly to matter. Rejecting the quantum in favor of plain mechanics.

And matter was the medium. But the energy of data was the force.

His personal exegesis of the eternal, his eternity theory, subsumed the human and organic into a position on the ascendance of energy. As a fuel and dynamic, but also as the very definition of life. Into which all categories of the previously-defined-as-living were necessarily subsumed. So that life was no longer understood as merely biological but as a flowing stream—atomic movement, regardless of the capacity for subjective awareness. Or emotion.

Indifferent to all the animals, human or otherwise, and their puny declarations of uniqueness.

His work hearkened back to the thought of the ancients, where the sun and other elementals were personified. Deified. And worshipped accordingly. But it was a far vaster hermeneutics, enfolding aspects of Buddhism and the transcendental. Erasure of the self, the crossing of boundaries. Both pre- and post-humanist—death and extinction were concept illusions.

And therefore unthreatening, in his body of work. History, present, and future mapped out a transference of energy into more efficient and thus more perfect forms.

Some of his fellow academics were intimidated, predictably. One called his thought-cycle "icy cold."

To soften that alleged frigidity, when he was on the lecture circuit, he relied on metaphors and anecdotes. The human was a vessel for the energetic, he liked to say. When he presented eternity in basic dualistic terms, his audience felt comforted.

Energy could be read as spirit, then. Seen in a continuum with religion. Rather than in opposition to it.

In fact it was the secular materialists who gave him the most pushback. The odd phenomenologist. And the socialists with their utopian delusions and small-farming fantasies.

To divorce the notion of cognition from physicality, sentience from the empirical experience of the body, or intrinsic value from systems of labor and power hegemonies was scientifically bankrupt and politically dangerous, they argued. Respectively.

Yawn.

Della didn't read his work except for interviews on websites. Places like *Wired* or *io9*. Then she'd bring up some half-baked objections. Like, why would anyone choose to be pure energy?

"You're missing the point, hon," he'd say. "It's not a question of choosing."

"If you offered to take away my body and let me exist as a stream of energy instead, I'd be all, Fuck you very much," she said. "*Everyone* would. Except people with chronic, debilitating pain, maybe. And a few quadriplegics."

"Isn't that ableist?"

"Shut up, Keith. I'm being serious, here."

"No one's taking away your body, hon. I'm very attached to it myself."

"But it seems like you're saying it'd be good," she pressed. "Like you *want* it."

"The theory isn't prescriptive. It's *descriptive*. It describes an arc. Historically, post-Second Industrial Revolution, and into post-post–modernity. In terms of our trajectory. As a cultural pluriverse engulfed in an information juggernaut. Where the ongoing transformation from tangible-goods trading, in economic transactions, to energy as the generative value has been accelerating, on a roughly exponential curve, since before the formulation $E = mc^2$ even . . ."

"Jesus, Keith. What*ever*."

She was patting at her face with circular pads.

Cotton Rounds, said the bag they came out of. A tube of white disks. Part of her evening cleansing routine, which consisted of exactly ten steps. Each involving a different product from a bottle, a pot, or—in the case of the horrific Korean face masks that made her look like the guy in *Friday the 13th*—a foil packet.

In her own line of work—planning big-ticket events for networks and streamers, galleries and museums—the revenue was feast or famine. They'd depended on his income, recently. Since, at the height of the pandemic, she'd had to go virtual, where the money sucked.

It had gotten better, but it wasn't as before. Still, she hung out with the glitterati from time to time. Flew back and forth between LA and New York and had worked the Met Gala three years in a row.

He liked being her plus-one.

"What I see is, when you talk about that stuff, it's like you relish it. Like you admire this, whatever! This conversion. Like energy is the new god. Which is, as far as I can tell, completely depressing."

"It's not a new god, Della. It's the old god. The always-already god. Seen in a revolutionary light."

He wished they hadn't gone for the his-and-hers sinks. Didn't like to bust out the nose-hair trimmer in mixed company.

Also, there was something he was grappling with and needed to process. Ideally, in silence. He was on the horns of a dilemma.

One of his colleagues, a blowsy middle-aged woman named Trudy who resented his prestige, had unearthed a paper he'd written years ago, as a skinny post-doc living on Top Ramen, and compared it to something she'd read by someone else.

Gilles Deleuze, to be precise. She said there was an unattributed quotation. Word for word.

The original was famous, so there was no room for ambiguity, she'd said, and taken a highlighter to his article. Then a highlighter to the Deleuze text. In translation, of course. *Why do men fight for their servitude as stubbornly as though it were their salvation?*

He wanted to tell her he hadn't even read *Anti-Oedipus*, at that point in his evolution as a thinker, so how could it be plagiarism? Plus his work had nothing to do with Deleuze's metaphysics.

They existed in different strings of the multiverse. Side by side but rarely touching.

When he saw the quote highlighted, in Deleuze and in his own paper, his first thought was: convergence! He pictured how, for a split second in the process of his composition, the neurons pulsing through his body had moved along the same wave as Deleuze's.

Waves and particles. Like harmonics in physics. Was he getting that right? Sinusoidal waves?

Maybe not. He forgot.

But A, to admit he hadn't read Deleuze when he'd already had his doctorate would be humiliating.

And 2, *had* he read Deleuze? Back then?

It wasn't impossible. Sometimes he'd gone to the classic brands for source material. And no, he wasn't always rigorous with footnotes. Allowed himself to be transported—broad gestures and sweeping cerebrations. That transport was a sign of genius.

Anyway, appropriation was a tried-and-true modality. Everything was repetition now, all art only mimesis, all thought only a reconfiguration of existing data. Sampling was fine when the hip-hop guys did it, wasn't it? Or the collagists. Visual artists like the Kienholzes of yore. Hell, even Martin Luther King Jr.! His plagiarism, now, was a postscript no one mentioned. To do so would be an insult to his memory. And to all African Americans.

We stand on the shoulders of giants. Reach even farther toward the heavens. Building our Tower of Babel.

Our Colossus of Rhodes.

Trudy and her small-minded colleagues refused to collapse art into criticism. Or vice versa. Mired in outmoded, irrelevant categories.

She'd come to him, he had to give her some credit for that. Before taking bureaucratic action. She'd said, "I want to afford you the opportunity to marshal your defenses."

It had been decent, on her part. She could have kept it to herself, then blindsided him at a faculty meeting.

Seen in a strategic light, though, that kind of decency was naïve. His impulse was to fight fire with fire. To persuade her to stand down. Surely, in one of her own publications—far less plentiful than his—she'd done some opportunistic passage-lifting too?

But no suspicious passages leapt out as he skimmed them. It

made him wish he'd read the old masters. Instead of secondaries and synopses. For all he knew she'd cut and pasted from Freud. Changing a pronoun here and there. He wouldn't have caught it. If it wasn't well-digitized and easily searchable, anyway. He didn't read words printed on wood pulp—never entered a library. It was a personal creed. They were nothing but cemeteries, full of monuments to the dead.

So fighting fire with fire was off the table. His second choice had been a personal attack. Ad hominem.

He'd done some research, but at first all he'd come up with was a post on social that referred lightly, in passing, to her WASP ancestry. Could be seen as evidence of hegemonic bias—whiteness as a casual weapon of privilege, etc.—but being white himself, more's the pity, he couldn't do much with it.

He decided to sound out an Asian colleague.

In his own age cohort—a millennial, like him. They bonded over the pitiful social posts of older faculty members.

He sent him a link to it. Saying, *But this is OK, right?*

The colleague shrugged it off. *Seems innocuous*, he texted. *She was just joking. It's self-deprecating.*

Kind of a humblebrag, Keith texted back. *About whiteness.*

Still, he was inspired. You had to play a trump card, in the culture wars. And in the current climate, that card was racism. Plagiarism was a petty misdemeanor, racism a felony. In the card deck of identity crimes, being a copycat was maybe a 4 or 5. Then sexism, say a 7 or 8. Only a face card if it involved groping on a casting couch or the trafficking of minors.

Atop them all sat race. It was the ace. The ace of race.

He found a post with a picture of old albums from her eighties music collection. With a comment about cover design. One was a single called "Turning Japanese." Before his time, though he'd heard it. *No sex, no drugs, no wine, no women.* A power-pop ditty about a guy in a jail cell missing his girlfriend, but you could stake out a racism claim for sure.

It was the title and the chorus, for Chrissake. Candy from a baby.

He couldn't bring the second post to Tony Lee's attention. At that point it would look like a vendetta. So he pointed Tony to another post of hers, some random image from her kitchen of a cockroach standing on a pile of unwashed dishes. Didn't critique the crappy housekeeping: antifeminist.

Instead he dressed it up as solidarity. *I so identify with this*, he typed. *Look! She has Gregor Samsa for a guest.*

But scrolling through her posts, sure enough, Tony saw the Turning Japanese image.

He wasn't outraged. He was relaxed. But he did send her an email. Maybe a Content Warning should have been included, he suggested.

Keith wasn't bcc'd. But true, true, she apparently wrote back to Tony.

Went in and annotated her post. Put in the Content Warning. A minor, civil exchange. Disappointing.

But still, a small piece of ammunition he might need. He couldn't "marshal" any "defenses" on a strictly textual basis. So he just said to her pleasantly, over drinks at a depressing retirement party for some ancient fossil, that he certainly hadn't *intended* to quote Deleuze without citing him. He was *absolutely* willing to publish not a retraction but a *revision* of the article, now including the citation.

Beside the appetizer table, she looked at him with her mouth hanging open.

Not attractive.

Then, the very next day, went whining to Admin.

So now he'd been called into the dean's office. Which was a place you didn't want to be summoned to.

If the dean wanted to schmooze, it'd be an invitation to lunch. Or cocktails, best-case scenario. Her office wasn't the setting for schmoozing. It was a stage for takedowns.

And he was coming up for tenure in the fall but didn't have it yet. The arrows in his quiver were, 1, a mediocre offer from Yale and a cushy offer from MIT, where the kids played with their Transformers, and B, an upcoming appearance on *The Daily Show* to stump for his new book. Which was already selling nicely.

Plus Trudy's Insta racism. That was it.

"You feel like fooling around?" he asked Della.

She had a thing she liked to do, a modified rape fantasy where she murmured, "No, don't do it. I'm a virgin. And you're so big. So huge. Don't put it in. I'll scream."

Dumb. But highly effective.

She sighed. "Fine. Just let me finish. Five minutes. I still have to tone and moisturize."

He wore beige cotton pants and dirty Crocs and a white tank top under an unbuttoned sky-blue shirt Della had bought him at the Prada store on Rodeo. Set off his tan.

Playing it casual. If he went in all buttoned up and formal, it'd be like an admission of guilt. A legitimation of the hierarchy, inter alia, and the structure of pandering social contracts it was based on.

He planned to discuss the ideology of intellectual property ownership, its morally bankrupt foundations in imperialist capitalism. In his own work capital was less an archvillain than a friendly midwife, of course.

But the dean, before she assumed her present sellout position as a figurehead and watchdog, had had Marxian leanings—studied under Fred Jameson.

When it came to Jameson, Keith enjoyed the lectures but couldn't read the prose. Hyper-referential. Encoded.

He felt like a kid, brought up in front of the principal for tagging school property. Or smoking in the stairwell. Was reminded strongly, pushing the heavy door open, of libraries.

The walls of the office were lined with books. Like so many guns in an armory.

Maybe that was a better simile than graveyards.

He smiled to himself. The library as armory. Walter Benjamin had probably covered it. Right? But still.

The dean presided over her moth-eaten tomes like a general over his nation's arsenal. Behold the might of information behind me, peasant! And despair!

Sitting in chairs before the ponderous oak desk, their backs to him as he went in, were three others.

He'd hoped for a one-on-one. Not even a month ago, the dean had plied him with drinks and dangled the possibility of a named chair. But this was an ambush.

His accuser, a suit he didn't know, and dammit, little Tony Lee. Et tu, Brute.

Maybe it was a good sign, though. Maybe Tony would go to bat for him.

The dean had a closed-up face.

She was a chameleon, turning color to match her surroundings. When she'd ordered up twenty-dollar mojitos for them both, her face had been animated by flickers of yellow and green.

The lucre of gold, the envy of others. Lit up and open.

Now it was mossy as the tomb.

Curtly she introduced him to the suit. An ombudsman. And lawyer. Intellectual property rights.

He had to pull a fourth chair over from where it was backed up against the wall—no one had bothered to set one up for him.

An elementary power play. He wouldn't fall for it.

He grabbed the back of the chair and swung it into place.

Almost exuberant. Like, Whoa, here's a great chair to sit on! What a find!

"I'll cut right to the chase," she said when he was seated. "This is a code-blue situation, Keith. We'll be needing a public apology. A press release with a heartfelt mea culpa. Also, a pledge from you to donate the proceeds from the new book to a literacy organization. All of them. Failing that, the repercussions will have to be severe."

"Hold on," he said, leaning forward with a jolt. Shocked, he had to admit, and trying not to show it. The hairs on the back of his neck prickled. *All* the proceeds? He still had to pay for the goddamn his-and-hers sinks. "Uh . . . that's extreme, don't you think? Wouldn't we be making a mountain out of a molehill?"

"It's already a mountain," said the dean. "It's an erupting volcano. The falling ash could blanket the citadel. And smother us all. You're part of the brand, Keith. Not some anonymous adjunct. So your job is to help us drive on past that erupting volcano and put the fiery magma in the rearview mirror. And that's it."

"It's not ideal, I realize," he said. "But I mean, this happened, what, twelve years ago? Before I was even here. It's ancient history. I was a glorified student. A mere boy of twenty-five. The age of Keats when he died!"

"Are you kidding me with this?"

"A youthful indiscretion," he said. "Back then I barely believed in attribution. Hey! I was a libertarian."

"That's certainly unfortunate. And I grieve for you. But your personal politics are hardly germane."

"How about a compromise? I simply *talk* to the editors of the journal, say I've discovered the oversight—"

"Well, *I* discovered it," said Trudy mildly.

"—and ask them to publish a corrected version? If they say yes, which they may *well*, due to the added value of having my name in their minor publication right when *Eternity* is hitting the non-fiction bestseller lists, much better for the university. And that way, we *all* win."

"Incorrect," said the dean. "They won't bite. They're not idiots. The only way we win is the mea culpa, Keith. We have to own it. We, as a hallowed institution of higher learning that strives to mold the moral character of young persons, and you, as a trusted employee of that institution. Shameful and penitent. Admitting your wrongdoing. Making a clean breast of it. And a fresh start."

He glanced sidelong at his accuser. And Tony.

Trudy looked calm. As a stagnant pond.

Tony looked embarrassed.

The lawyer was checking his phone. Bored.

"Listen," he said. "This is hardcore. Isn't there some wiggle room here? Collegial fellow feeling? Can't you at least let me *approach* the journal? In a spirit of moderation? Before we go straight to the nuclear option?"

Tony shifted uncomfortably. "We want the best outcome for everyone. But you know how it is. You can't just go around stealing."

"It could be worse, believe me," said the dean. "This is us giving you a chance. So man up, Keith."

It had gone down so fast he hadn't had a chance to play his ace. His ace of race. Hadn't broached the subject of Yale or MIT, either. Could he nail down one of the offers? In a hurry?

He'd said to the firing squad, Give me a week. For the press release. To get my ducks in a row with the publicists.

"Three days is my best offer," said the dean.

He could see moving back East. Get away from the wildfires. The unhealthy air and freeway traffic. If they sold the condo now, the renovations would be paid for.

But he couldn't nail down Yale or MIT in three days. They'd smell a rat if he was in a sudden rush. His hallmark was autonomy. Strength. And the leviathans moved slowly, creaking like water mills.

They wanted him now, but they wouldn't want him after the news flash. And the bowing and scraping. Those offers would be rescinded faster than you could say Jack Robinson. As dear Dad used to put it. Between enthusiastic cuffings.

Down the road, maybe he'd move over to the private sector. Probably a better fit. The private sector didn't have these stodgy ethics. Or any.

He could go in as a dark horse when he eventually went corporate. A dark horse raging against the fusty old machine. Galloping into the new one. His mane afire.

But right now he had to tell Della.

He got out a bottle of wine. Wine was the way to her heart.

She'd taken her high heels off and was sitting on the couch flexing her toes.

"So something's happened, Della. I'm gonna have to eat shit."

"Excuse me?"

"A long time ago I made a mistake. Left out a footnote in a paper I wrote. Someone dusted it off, a middle-aged woman who's jealous of my success, and now the college is pissed. I have to do damage control. Say I transgressed in a press release and bend the knee. It's gonna be ugly."

"Damage control? For a *footnote*?"

"It looks like I was stealing. The other scholar's quotation."

"Was it important?"

"Not central to my thesis. Just a piece of language. Connective tissue. A couple of sentences."

"You have to do a press release? About a missing footnote? Like, who *cares*?"

"You've heard of plagiarism, right? It's that. I mean, it *wasn't*—it was an unconscious act of repetition—but it looks like it was. And you can't prove a negative. The optics are bad."

She accepted a glass of the wine.

"The worse news is, I have to donate the royalties from the book. To some educational charity. As restitution. A gesture of apology."

She set down her goblet on the coffee table in a hurry. Bang. Almost cracked the glass.

"Keith. Are you for real?"

He shrugged.

"You have to pay, what, hundreds of thousands of dollars? For leaving out a footnote?"

"Looks like it."

"Is this before or after *The Daily Show*?"

"Uh, yeah. Before."

"But will you still be on it? I told, like, all my friends."

"Doubtful. I'd have to say, probably not. No."

She stared at him.

"I'll be a black sheep for a hot minute. In the academy. No getting around it."

"This is crazy. Like, there's climate change going on. And wars! Children in Sudan! And Ukraine!"

"Indeed."

"A press release! And maybe half a million dollars! For a *footnote*?"

He nodded sadly. "That's the world we live in."

She let him have sex with her. After some commiseration.

But she stayed quiet, during. There was nothing in there about him being huge.

He noted the absence.

His publisher, it turned out, wasn't on board. There was a long meeting the next morning. Their position was, he should resign today. Just walk away. If he did, there'd be no reason for a PR. The university wouldn't have to save face, and chances were better than even that they wouldn't take any action.

After all, it wouldn't be good for them. To call attention to an original sin when he wasn't even on the faculty.

Meanwhile the book, which represented a significant projected revenue stream as well as a considerable investment on the part of the publisher, would keep selling.

"This isn't a Me Too situation," said the editor-in-chief. "In that case, we'd go nuclear too. You don't have any Me Too skeletons in your closet, do you?"

"My closet's Me Too skeleton-free."

Although: you never knew.

"But this is a minor matter of a missing footnote in an academic journal from 2013—was it?—that maybe fifty people ever read. Look, just run a little cost-benefit analysis. Back of the envelope. You forgo what, low six figures? Annually? In lost salary. And yeah, you have to foot the bill for your own health insurance. But you recoup that loss at least threefold, we estimate, in the first year. And we keep the TV appearances. And radio."

"But what about my credibility?"

"You get to keep that too. Better not to be a professor than to be one standing in the corner. Wearing a dunce's cap."

"And what's my reason? For resigning?"

"So this is what we suggest," put in his publicist. "You're starting a nonprofit. A 501(c)(3). You loved teaching, but this is a new chapter. Because what you love even more is giving back. In the real world. To an even larger community."

"A think tank?"

"Pick your poison. It could be, like, creative solutions to fossil fuel dependency. Bringing distributed rooftop solar to BIPOC, frontline, and low-wealth communities. You know—energy-related, innovative, and forward-looking. *You* choose the mandate. And what you're going to do, with the proceeds from this book—though not *all* of them—is start up this organization. With young, passionate leaders. Fresh-faced wonks from Duke or Michigan. And maybe throw in some Historically Black Colleges and Universities."

"I mean, there won't be *that* much revenue."

"Doesn't matter. Seed money. You can raise more funds through the philanthropists. And entrepreneurs. Elon's a fan, right? He tweeted it."

"The internet *despises* Elon. The young internet, anyway."

"Point is, even if it fails or quietly founders, you still get credit for trying."

"Huh," he said.

Wished it had been his own idea.

He tendered the resignation by email. Effective immediately, it said. Apologized for the inconvenience, but his TAs could finish out the semester. They had the syllabi in hand and had done the reading.

He was deeply grateful for the opportunity, he wrote, and held the university, his colleagues, and his students in high esteem. As they held him (he embedded a link to ratemyprofessors.com: the kids didn't use it much, but the faculty hadn't found the platforms they did use).

Unfortunately, at this exciting juncture, he felt he needed to move on. Briefly he outlined his plan for the nonprofit.

"Yes!" said Della, standing at his shoulder as he pressed Send. "So can you still be on *The Daily Show*? Now?"

It wasn't a done deal. The dean might still launch her torpedo.

"Remains to be seen," he said.

But the email was met with a deafening silence. Except for a message from the department secretary saying his resignation had been received and the paperwork was in progress.

Also, inviting him to come remove his personal effects and tender his keycards and credentials.

At your earliest convenience, she wrote. Thank you.

They didn't even put up a fight. It was insulting, frankly.

And therefore, a vindication. They didn't deserve him.

He didn't want to set foot in the mildewed halls again. There be dragons. But he had to get his stuff. He kept a signed first edition of *Cryptonomicon* on his desk. To impress the students. And on the wall, a Damien Hirst print.

He thought about sending Della to take care of it. Put out a feeler. She refused flatly.

"Well, how about your new assistant?" he asked. "That homely one. With the Invisalign."

"No way. It'd be completely unprofessional," she said.

He picked a low-traffic day, the Friday after his email, and drove over late in the afternoon. He had to see the secretary to hand over his cards, so it needed to be before she left at five thirty.

He took care of that first—she was a boxy, rodent-faced woman who ate microwaved pasta at her desk and barely acknowledged him—and then picked up the first edition, the print, and his Vicodin stash. He'd sacrifice the rest.

Let them paw through his leavings. Dumpster divers.

Making his way along the corridor with his box, as fast as he could go without breaking into a sprint, he saw an office door open ahead of him.

Tony Lee. Who turned and locked eyes with him.

Nothing for it. He had to slow down.

"Oh, wow," said Tony. "You're really leaving."

"Well, what the hell," he said, standing there with his box pressed to his chest. Cradling it like a newborn. "Greener pastures. Maybe."

"I'm sorry to see you go," said Tony.

"Yeah, but. It was the right thing."

Tony cocked his head. "The *right* thing?"

"You know. You gotta feel like your colleagues have your back."

"I guess you do," said Tony, smiling. "Honor among thieves."

Glint of steel, he thought, walking past and away.

The smooth, hard glint of steel.

INSURRECTIONIST

J onah liked to mention his record collection, which he called "my vinyl," and wore a heavy chain hanging from one belt loop, holding his keys and a bottle opener. Aka "my trusty churchkey." He'd whip it out in the break room to crack open a probiotic seltzer. With what he obviously thought was manly flair.

But if you wanted to show off a manly, bottle-opening flair, it had to be with beer. Not probiotic seltzer.

He also wore a T-shirt with a picture of the Sasquatch on the front and on the back the legend HE IS REAL. Another one in heavy rotation showed monkeys floating in space in astronaut helmets. Their faces were angry. And he had a soul chip: he was an aging hipster. She knew this because he liked to remark on it.

"Ha ha, I'm just an aging hipster."

Whenever he said something condescending, which was often, she'd make a mental retort. Once she'd made a retort out loud, but then he'd acted wounded. Grievously injured, like she'd gotten him all wrong. Even his woundedness was condescending.

He was the kind of boss who pretended not to be a boss but

secretly got off on it. Reminded her of Les, sometimes. Not physically, of course. Les hadn't had facial hair or worn Sasquatch tees. But they had condescension in common.

You couldn't get ahead of Jonah. All you could do was try to hold your own. Achieve a footing of equality. Or equity, which they talked about in the trainings he rolled his eyes at when he thought no one was looking. They were a citywide, interoffice mandate: DEI. Diversity, Equity, and Inclusion.

During the trainings he jiggled one knee. He sat back in his seat, in the chair circle, and nodded. Crossed his arms, then uncrossed them. His body language said: I'm fronting like I'm relaxed, but I'm deeply defensive.

If he'd asked her advice, which he never did, she would have said, It's easy. Just don't cross your arms or jiggle your knee. Those are called tells.

The consultants had him dead to rights. He was compelled to admit it: equity was the goal. Urban planning might be the task at hand, but the larger goal was equity.

The mouth moved. It said, Go equity! Equity onboarding!

But so did the knee.

And it said, This is such bullshit.

When she'd seen Les again, more than a year after he dumped her, he'd been sitting in her uncle's favorite diner. Eating a burger with a group of her uncle's drinking buddies—the ones her aunt didn't like. He'd known one of them since grade school. "They're a little *rough*, Wiff," her aunt said. Her uncle didn't invite them to the barbecues so she never saw them, usually.

But there he'd been. After all those months, he turned out

to be a guy *her own uncle* hung out with. Even though Les was, like, twenty years younger. Or maybe fifteen. Who knew if he'd told her his real age back when they were dating? He'd told her a fake name.

But her uncle had said his real name: Les.

The name of his street had also been mentioned, after he got up and left. While her uncle and his friends were shaking their heads and talking it over. And her uncle was patting her back and rubbing it.

He thought the patting would comfort her, but it only made her feel more abject. And keep crying. She'd wanted to shrug off the hand but didn't want to hurt his feelings.

Her uncle had said his full name, Les Rosario. And that he lived in a small house in Silver Lake that used to be his grandmother's. One of her uncle's friends had said: "Not Silver Lake. Adjacent. Old Filipinotown. It's on Rampart, I think?"

So his name would be on the title transfer, she guessed.

She ran a title search at work. And there it was.

She wasn't the only one, her uncle's drinking buddies said. There had to be other women he'd dumped and lashed out at. He was always bragging about his scores.

"Maybe he's borderline," her uncle had suggested. "They have a hard time forming lasting attachments. It may be out of his control. Like, compulsive."

"He obviously has anger-management issues," said her aunt when Letty told her about it. "If you break up with someone, even if it's just a short relationship, you should never make it about *them*. It's just about the two of you. Whether your energies are in sync."

Her aunt talked about feng shui. Her solution to anger or

frustration was always self-care. Or rearranging your furniture, plants, or lighting. The solution was adjusting your personal surroundings.

But if you saw your personal surroundings as not just your house or apartment but the whole city, maybe the feng shui approach applied to Les too. And the equity goal.

Because equity meant justice, where people got what they deserved. In the trainings that was positive, since black and gay and poor folks deserved more love and money. But it was also negative, which they didn't exactly stipulate in the trainings but was obviously true. White, straight guys like Les deserved less love and money. (And OK, he wasn't totally white, but he totally passed. Never told anyone he was one-quarter Asian.)

It was a zero-sum game. And she couldn't take Les's money, but maybe she could make him feel less loved.

Ever since the diner episode, he was like a splinter in her thumb. She tried to pry it out, but it just went in deeper. She remembered his expression when she saw him sitting there and had to confront him. He'd raised his hands, in the booth, like he was innocent. "I've never even met her," he'd said.

And expected them to buy it. That he literally wasn't him.

That was what bothered her the most. His confidence that he could pull it off. That he could gaslight her. And all of them.

His face, fake-innocent and startled, showed up in her dreams.

In one dream that face hovered with balloons around it. Not party balloons but hot-air balloons, with baskets hanging beneath.

Another time the face showed up on the body of a lion. One of those hybrid monsters from mythology. Or Harry Potter. Like a griffin or a sphinx. The lion-man was walking along a runway with people watching from below. But somehow the runway was in a bakery. Where they made cinnamon buns and the lines of cinnamon were powdered blood. She knew that, in the dream. Not from how they looked but from a word that came to her. *Blood.*

They'd only dated for fourteen weeks. Every Thursday after they connected on OkCupid. He couldn't do weekends, he said, because of his job and workout schedule. But in between they'd texted a lot. He sent her cute GIFs and compliments. Called her Little Bird. And My Fuzzy Chick.

Sickening.

Even then she hadn't been into the fuzzy chick endearment. She wasn't a baby bird and didn't wish to be, but she'd overlooked the cringe factor. Let it wash past her in a wave of endorphins. A surge of excitement. She'd had *such* a crush on him.

People say dumb things, she'd told herself, when they're crushing. She'd seen it as a sign that he was into her.

He was handsome, as well as buff. A show-off about his body, always walking around her apartment without a shirt. Not just after sex, but also before. He'd take off his shirt early on and lounge around with a bare chest before they got in bed.

He'd say, "It's so hot in here. I'm burning up."

Though she kept the AC at 72.

She was the opposite, wrapping herself in a sheet just to stand up and go to the bathroom.

That was how the Little Bird thing started.

"Look at you. Carrying your whole nest with you. You don't have to be ashamed of your *body*, Little Bird."

"Yes I do," she'd said.

"Well, it looks good from where I'm sitting."

But he ghosted her after fourteen weeks. She'd kept texting

him, making excuses to herself about why he wasn't answering—
also, now, sickening—and finally he wrote back.

Sorry, but you're just too fat for me.

The first time she drove by his house, on her lunch break, she
didn't stop. It was only twelve minutes from the office on surface
streets. She slowed down and scoped it out—a modest bungalow
with a neat front yard. Bare, but neat. Right then, an empty
driveway. He had to be at work.

His neighbors, too. No cars at their houses either.

The next lunch break she cased the joint. Like a burglar. She
parked down the block, put on sunglasses and a baseball cap with
her hair pulled back, and grabbed an empty Chipotle bag she'd
left in the backseat. Figured she'd look like she was delivering
food for an app.

It was a nine-to-five neighborhood. Almost all the driveways
were empty.

No security cameras. The front windows were large but had
those ugly vertical blinds. Beige vinyl. Around the side were his
trash cans.

The third time she went over she walked down the narrow
garbage lane and into the backyard. A punching bag hung from
a tree. EVERLAST. There was a lounge chair with tanning lotion
on the ground beside it. Not sunscreen, but actual *tanning* lotion.
So 1986!

The back door had small windows on either side. No blinds.
She looked through one into a kitchen. Saw a blender on the
counter with a big plastic canister beside it.

The label said KAGED MUSCLE.

He drank protein shakes, she remembered him telling her, to help maintain his bulk.

She tried the back-door knob, expecting nothing.

But it turned. The door opened. Surprise!

She stood there, conflicted. If she went in, she was a criminal. A young urban-planning professional turned into a felon.

Breaking and entering. Or trespassing, at least—she wouldn't break anything.

In the cop shows, if a door was unlocked, sometimes they went right in. But they were cops. And on TV.

Herself, she'd changed apartments since they dated. And her place was just a rental. He had no idea where she lived now. So she had that going for her. An advantage.

She heard a bird chirping.

Maybe it was a sign. The spirit of Little Bird.

Who'd been shot out of her nest.

So she went in, hands shaking from nervousness.

Mostly it was bland. No security cameras inside either. Just a ton of fitness equipment. Mirrors in every room except the kitchen.

Except for being a home gym, it didn't have much personality. Like a robot lived there.

The only personal thing she found was a small photo in a frame. Of an old Asian lady smiling.

His grandmother, it must be. Mima. Who'd passed before they met. Like her parents.

That part had been true, apparently.

The photo stood on a chest of drawers in the bedroom.

She thought, I hope you were a bitch. Because if you were nice, there's no excuse for him.

Then she felt bad about thinking bitch. Because honestly, Mima *did* look nice. She had a kind face.

And she had passed on.

I'm sorry, she amended in her head. I just meant, I hope there's a good reason he's like this.

She took a picture of it with her phone. A picture of a picture. Up close. As high-res as she could get. From the front and even the back.

On her way out the back door again, she saw a row of key hooks on the wall. With a cluster of keys on each one. On impulse, she tried one of them in the back door.

It worked. And on the same hook were two copies of it.

Was he the type to notice?

She wasn't sure. The place was tidy, so maybe. On the other hand, who didn't misplace a key?

She pocketed one of them.

She'd watched a video on YouTube, from an art museum, where a lady, the artist, just sat across from people.

And looked at them without speaking. For a very long time.

A few people started to laugh nervously, after several minutes. Others broke down crying. Some did both.

The art piece was subversive, said the comments. A gesture of social rebellion.

That was what she would do. A social rebellion, using art.

The photo wasn't hard to copy, and the frame was plain—she found it online and bought a bunch of them.

She parked around the block. Assembled her disguise. It'd be a different one every visit. This time she carried a pizza box. Sunglasses again, a KN95 on her face, and her hair in a scarf.

The back door was locked, but she opened it with her key. A copy from the hardware store. She put his own key back on the hook. And stood the duplicate photo on the bathroom counter, next to the sink. So that he'd see it when he sat down on the toilet. Or went in to brush his teeth.

On her way out, she put the pizza box in his recycling bin. Scrunched down beneath some corrugated cardboard. That way he wouldn't notice unless he went looking.

Two lunches later she went back. Carrying a grocery bag, wearing a cowboy hat with her hair up inside it and a bandanna over her mouth. In the bathroom, the photo was unmoved.

And the original, in the bedroom, was still there too.

She put another duplicate on the kitchen counter.

Eventually he'd change the locks. Or set up cameras.

Leave no trace, they said when you went camping. So she left no trace. Not even in the recycling. Wiped down the photo frame and the back-door knob when she left. The bin with the pizza box, she saw, had already been emptied.

The next time she went—she always did a drive-by first, to make sure—his car was parked out front. Not in the driveway, but on the street. Across from his house.

But she recognized it: an Audi he kept perfectly detailed. She'd only ridden in it once, but they'd made out for a while and she'd seen how spotless it was.

She kept on driving.

He couldn't stay home forever, though. He worked in an office park. His job had to do with sales—"collaborative and real-time"—and depended on the office network. They weren't set up for remote work yet, he'd said. Behind the curve. In their tech.

Still, after that she was more anxious. Walked slowly and quietly. Checked for new cameras.

And carried pepper spray in her pocket. Just in case.

She could have brought someone as backup. One of the other junior planners, Ginny or Lewis. They might've been up for it. Lewis used to play pranks on Jonah, retro kid stuff like handshake buzzers and whoopee cushions. Ironically stupid, he said.

None of them had any respect for Jonah, but Lewis couldn't stand him. Due to a performance review during which Jonah had used the phrase *learned helplessness.*

Jonah had given him a talking-to after the third whoopee cushion incident. "It's still harassment," he'd said. "Even when the victim is your supervisor."

Jonah got red in the face after that incident: it had occurred during a meeting with some Caltrans bureaucrats and a rich developer they'd never met before.

In Lewis's defense, he hadn't been told the developer was going to be present. None of the junior staff were told.

Because legally, he wasn't supposed to be.

"You undermined the credibility of the whole department," Jonah said. "With your puerile harassment."

"Really? What kind of harassment *was* it?" asked Lewis. "It wasn't sexual. Or gender. Or racist. Or religious. You can't have harassment without a category."

"That's true, Jonah," said Ginny. "There's no such thing as general harassment. It was in the training video."

"There should be," said Jonah.

"Well, there isn't," shrugged Lewis.

"It's a microaggression, then," said Jonah.

"Microaggressions have to have categories too," said Lewis.

"The exact same categories," agreed Ginny.

Finally Jonah conceded, "OK, maybe it's not harassment. By the book. But it's certainly inappropriate workplace behavior."

"So jokes are inappropriate?" asked Lewis.

"You said it," said Jonah.

He thought he was funny, though his own jokes were always weak puns and you had to force a smile. But for a while after the meeting, if he cracked a joke, Lewis would shake his head regretfully and go, "I'm sorry, but I can't laugh. It's inappropriate."

Ginny had said she hated Les herself, after Letty showed her the text. She struggled with eating issues too. Cycled through diets: low-carb, Mediterranean, WeightWatchers, paleo, raw foods.

Ginny would have come with her to Les's if she'd asked. But she didn't feel like explaining.

Her final visit would be the climax. She had almost a dozen photos left, and she'd set them up on every surface. In his living room, dining room, bedroom. Everywhere he looked, when he came home one day, there would be Mima. Smiling at him.

The uprising of a ghost. By a ghosted.

But she hesitated. With the rest of the photos sitting in her trunk.

Would he be afraid it was supernatural? Even for a split second? He wasn't the type to believe in spirits. He didn't have a religion, for example. And she didn't either.

But once he'd said to her, "If I can't see it, it doesn't mean shit."

She'd said, "How about radiation? Or gravity?"

"Well, you *can* see those," he'd said. "What they do, anyway. But why are we talking about this, Little Bird? You know what *I'd* like to see?"

Turned out to be her. Going down on him.

She should have walked away right then.

The rule with blowjobs was, if a guy steered you down, exerting even the lightest pressure with his hand on your head, you should think twice. It wasn't about consent when you were already having sex. But it was still about power.

And politeness.

You should think twice. And the second thought should be, no.

When he saw the army of Mimas, would he know it was her?

He might.

But what if he blamed someone else?

Maybe she'd set off a chain reaction.

She went to the monthly barbecue at her aunt and uncle's. She was always invited, though she didn't always attend. Since her parents had died her uncle liked to keep tabs on her. They had a pool and a yard so big there was room for a pool, a ramada with a pizza oven and a wide-screen TV, a trampoline and treehouse for their two kids, and a vegetable garden. Organic. That a gardener took care of.

She volunteered to help serve up burgers. Stood beside her uncle at the grill as he dumped patties on plates with a spatula and they both breathed in the smoke. Her eyes watered.

"You know that guy?" she said. "Les? Who was so mean to me?"

"Of course I do."

"Do you still see him? Ever?"

"No way. We cut him off. I wouldn't do you that way, sweetie."

"I was just wondering. What he's up to."

Her uncle stood with a patty on his spatula, midair.

"Why would you care? You shouldn't *ever* think of him, Letty. He's an a-hole. A nobody."

"I know. It's not that I want to be in touch. I'm just wondering what ended up happening with him."

"And you have that—you're still seeing that young fella who went to Princeton, right? The one who works for that panda-logo outfit?"

"Oak leaves. Not pandas. It's all good. He's abroad for a couple of weeks. In Sweden and Finland. Forest transects."

"Well, he's got get-up-and-go. That kid's a real keeper."

"Wait. Put down the patty. Here." She shoved the plate under the spatula.

Her uncle was easily distracted. Not a multitasker.

He flipped the burger onto it.

"I like him a lot," she went on. "But that's a different subject. I want to know what happened to that guy. Les."

"Why? Why would you want to know anything *about* him?"

"I just want to know if he's gotten in trouble yet," she said. "OK? For the way he treats women."

"Ah," said her uncle. He inclined his head. "*I* see."

"Can't you get someone to make inquiries?"

"Um . . ."

"Like Brendan? He was a policeman, right?"

"Well. Les never ran afoul of the *law*. That I know of."

"I just mean, Brendan's kind of tough. He's like, your tough-guy friend. He used to be a boxer. Didn't he?"

"Malone? Well, not professionally. But yeah. When we were kids he did a few fights. He still goes to a boxing gym."

"So maybe he could, like, reach out to him. Pretend to be friendly. And just see how he's doing."

"I'll think about it."

"Please?"

"I'll put out a couple of feelers. You satisfied?"

"If you do, I will be."

"OK. Fine. Fine, fine, fine."

She put down the plate and threw her arms around him. "You're the best."

Even when Deacon was back from being in-country—that was how they put it, at his work—he was still far away. Lived in DC for his job. He'd grown up in LA, though, and they'd met at one of her uncle's barbecues, when he was visiting his family. His mother knew her aunt from hot yoga.

The distance was the hard part. Because of the time difference.

She did think about telling him. They'd FaceTime almost every night, once he was tucked in bed and she'd eaten, and describe how their days had gone. Moments. Problems. The moods they were in.

But she never mentioned what had happened with Les. Too humiliating.

And given how she looked now, Deacon might not really get it. How cutting it had been. Like a punch in the face.

He might even laugh, if she told him the line. And say, Well, yeah, that's a dick move for sure. But it's also just *stupid*.

And let's face it: stalking an ex, plus trespassing, would make her look unhinged.

So she kept the key in a shoebox. With her pink vibrator. And a tab of acid someone had handed her that she'd accepted but never taken. In the shape of a pig.

Her uncle called her at the office and asked if she wanted to get lunch. He liked to have lunch out. He didn't have a job, so he had plenty of time.

Sure, she said. She could barely wait.

She asked for half a sick day, which Jonah sighed at, and met him at a restaurant in Beverly Hills. It took him a while to get around to the subject.

You couldn't rush her uncle. Too much pot when he was young.

First he had to tell her about her aunt's flower-arranging business. She had a new client, a Chinese company that liked ikebana. Even though it was Japanese. She had to set up multiple arrangements in their hotel suite every day. It was running her ragged, he said. She barely had time for her Pilates and reiki.

Then he had to list off Reilly's latest successes on his track-and-field team. Her oldest cousin. Maybe sixteen now.

When people said entitled, Reilly was who they meant.

This year he'd taken on some hip-hop affectations. Though he was whiter than milk.

She felt restless, hearing about Reilly's shin splints even after they'd been served their meals.

"So what about the thing with Les?" she asked, when there was a pause in the monologue. "Did you get any information?"

Her uncle looked uncomfortable. "Some, I guess."

"Did Brendan talk to him?"

"They had a drink. Malone told him it was a one-off, though. Claimed he was going behind my back. Just to touch base again."

"And?"

"Thing is, sweetie, I don't think you're going to like it."

"Why? Tell me!"

"I guess he . . . well, he's engaged."

That stopped her. *Not* what she'd been expecting.

"To be *married*?"

Her uncle nodded. Munched on a forkful of salad.

"To who?"

"Uh, so, it's a woman who's a bit older. And, um . . ."

"Yeah?"

"Extremely well-off. He showed Malone a picture. Malone said, Bling bling bling. That she looked like a Kardashian. They're renting out the Hotel Bel-Air. For the wedding reception."

She could hardly believe it.

"He met her playing Dungeons & Dragons," added her uncle.

"What? *Les?* Playing D&D? Come on!"

"I guess she's a relative of one of the players' wives. Or a friend. Something."

"So, like, wait. He gets a happy ending?"

"See? This is why I didn't want to tell you."

She picked at her sweet-potato gnocchi.

"Maybe she's like, a mark. For him."

"A possibility. He told Malone he didn't have to sign a prenup. Pretty smug about it. And he's already moved in with her. Hardly ever goes back to his own place anymore. He's all set up at her mansion in the Palisades."

"Did Brendan say what her name was?"

"No. Or wait, yeah. The first name, anyway . . . could be Natasha? Or maybe Natalie. Natalya! That was it, I think."

"Just curious."

They ate in silence for a minute.

Hardly ever goes back to his own place anymore.

He'd probably never even *noticed* the three extra Mimas.

And he was going to be rich.

The love was still coming to him.

And now the money, too.

She browsed the hotel website and called from her office phone. Asked for the director of catering events. In regard to the Rosario wedding.

She got an assistant. Said she was an assistant, too—the wedding planner's assistant. She needed to double-check capacity. Some of the older people in the wedding party were still worried about COVID, she said. A few guests were unvaccinated. And immunocompromised.

"Swan Lake, correct?"

"Correct."

"Rosario-Kovalchuk? Let's see, three p.m.? March 11?"

"That's it."

"And you also have the Garden Ballroom. For rain and overflow."

"Right. It's the indoor capacity we're more concerned about."

"Let me get back to you, OK? What was that email again?"

She gave him an old one she never used. Yahoo. She already had what she needed.

Googled Natalya Kovalchuk. At first, not many matches. But when she googled Kovalchuk by itself, she got a ton of hits.

Yury Valentinovich Kovalchuk, an old associate of Vladimir Putin's, is rumored to be Putin's personal banker.

It might be a common name. In Russian there were naming rules she didn't know. A woman might not have the same last name as, say, her father. She wasn't sure. She'd only taken Spanish.

Deacon! she thought. She'd ask him. He had a Russian coworker. Or at least, formerly Russian. He talked about him a lot because he worked on Amur tigers and snow leopards. And Deacon had a thing for big cats. His own work was about the taiga and sustainability.

Super important, due to carbon sinks etc., but still, he said enviously. Pavel got to work on *cats*.

She didn't tell him the whole story—just that she had an ex who was a jerk. And now he was getting married. And his wife-to-be was, maybe, a rich Russian.

"I have a Teams meeting with Pavel tomorrow," said Deacon. "About the Finland stuff. Birch trees and Sami reindeer herders. Text me her name. I'll have a private Chat with him."

Holy shit, he texted the next day. *Do I have dirt for you.*

"Get this," he said on FaceTime. "Pavel *freaked out*. Asked if I was pulling his leg. He could barely believe it. Turns out she's famous over there. Or infamous. Closely related to an oligarch. We're talking the Russian mafia. Serious gangsters. Like, these could be the guys that bankrolled Trump. Back in the day. Letty! This woman might have *personally* seen the pee tape. That's how connected she is. I can't believe you used to *date* this guy!"

"I mean, it was just for a couple of months. Two years ago. He was a bodybuilder type. A poser."

"Well, he's gonna need those muscles. And maybe some Kevlar."

"He used to hang out with my uncle. He told a friend of theirs he didn't have to sign a prenup. He was proud of it."

"A *pre*nup? That's hilarious. These people don't bother with prenups. If he gets on the wrong side of *that* family, he'll end up dead in a ditch. Or riding around in a wheelchair. At best."

"So I shouldn't crash the wedding reception, you're saying."

"Ha *ha*. Don't go within a mile of it."

But when the wedding day arrived she found herself in a line of cars on the 405. Then winding up Stone Canyon Road.

She'd put on a cocktail dress and a pair of expensive shoes her aunt had handed down because they gave her blisters. Jimmy Choos. She'd never worn them before. She'd probably get blisters too. But she had to fit in. She'd added a pearl necklace and dangly pearl earrings from her mother. A pair of sunglasses with a chunky frame and a pink tint. And an actual wig.

Her hair was too recognizable. Where *did* you get that hair, her mother used to say. It wasn't white-person hair but kinky and springy and full. She had to use "ethnic" products to keep it under control. Even when she was in grade school. Her mother had always taken her to black beauty salons for her cuts. Because the white hairdressers didn't have a clue.

"It's like you had an affair," her dad had joked to her mom. "With a guy who had an Afro."

Her parents had both had flat, straight hair.

"Her hair is *beautiful*," her mother had said.

It was the tone of her mother's voice that she remembered most. How proud and protective.

Then they were gone, in five seconds of a semi jackknifing.

And now no one else would ever have that tone. When they talked to her. Or about her. It was gone.

Along with her mother.

At the hotel's guest parking, all the other cars had expensive logos. Between them her own car looked like it belonged in the staff lot.

She wended her way through the property, following the signs. Someone would stop her, probably. Ask for her invitation.

Then she'd say, Oh, I must have left it in my car. And just turn around and drive away again.

But no one did. There were so many partygoers she got lost in the crowd. A few were wearing masks, so she slipped her own out of her bag and put it on, too. Convenient.

Older, mostly. Deep tans, thick eyeliner, and heavy foundation. The kind of tacky, chunky jewelry that looked costume but probably wasn't.

Some were speaking Russian. She assumed.

Others were speaking English.

Along the edges of the crowd, she noticed guys just standing still. Wearing the same pinstriped dark suits. With earpieces in and thick necks.

Bodyguards. At a wedding.

One look, she told herself. One look at the couple. For closure.

A waiter passed with a tray of champagne and vodkas. Offered her the choice, so she took a flute. "For the first toast," he said.

Holding their drinks, people were turning to gaze in one direction. Toward a silvery gazebo.

She wished she wasn't so short. The heels didn't help—they sank into the grass. She moved through the throng to get closer.

Then she saw Les's head. And the head of a woman wearing a veil, pushed back from her face. She was as tanned as all the others. It was hard to tell what she looked like through the makeup. Long fake eyelashes. With a lot of mascara.

Les's face was the same. Still handsome. But too far away for her to make out the expression.

She edged closer, weaving between shoulders with her champagne flute held in front of her.

Trying to see his face better. What was it? That was different?

Maybe it was the stress of a wedding. Or being in front of so many people.

Because he was smiling, for sure. But when he'd smiled at her, back on those Thursday nights, it had been easy. Later she'd thought, that smile seemed so *real*. When all the time he was catfishing.

But this smile was more like—what was it like?

She stared. And then it hit her, finally.

It was like the fixed grin on one of those puppets people sat on their laps and pretended were talking. A ventriloquist's dummy.

The dummies' eyes were always too wide open. Like they were shocked forever.

Probably from having a puppeteer's hand up their ass.

He raised his glass and drank.

Then all the guests were repeating something. The same word. It sounded like Gorky. Or no, Gorko.

"Traditional," she heard someone murmur.

Les and the woman kissed. At the end, a bit confused. Like they didn't agree on when they should stop.

After he pulled away, she put her fingers up to her lips.

Worried about her lipstick being smeared, maybe.

But it wasn't smeared. Just gone. Except for a burgundy lip liner.

"Gorko, gorko, gorko."

Letty looked away. Swans floated on the pond.

The hotel must have clipped their wings. So they wouldn't fly off. Into traffic.

You couldn't have Swan Lake without the swans.

The setting should have felt idyllic—green lily pads and the water and the white, graceful birds.

But the tanned people shone with sweat and glittery makeup. Kept chanting and chanting. Like a mob.

"Gorko, gorko."

What does it mean? she thought.

She must have said it out loud.

The woman next to her sipped her champagne.

"Bitter. It means bitter."

THERAPIST

"**T**hat's just the new normal, folks," said a radio host.

She heard it constantly. Everything bad was referred to, with a jocular glibness, as the new normal.

ADHD. OCD. Depression. Agoraphobia. Xenophobia. Paranoia. Antisocial personality disorder. Most of the diagnoses in the DSM-5. Albeit often at a subclinical level.

Abnormality was the new normal.

"You know what it is?" said Stephanie over breakfast. "It's a long, collective moment of TI. Tonic immobility. A state of body paralysis induced by stress. A stress adaptation."

"I'm familiar with TI," Anne told her.

In humans, it was brought on by war. And rape.

"With some species," said Stephanie, forking up scrambled eggs, "it happens when they're about to be eaten by a predator. They may be simulating death as a defense mechanism. If the predator in question prefers live prey. Or they may be submitting. A neurological shutdown. Possibly for pain avoidance. I haven't read the scholarship. I'm just spitballing here."

"Really? But what's the evolutionary advantage of submitting to your own death?"

She struggled to chew a bite of slimy egg. Stephanie liked to undercook them.

"Passivity's kind of a stress adaptation, too. Right? Cynicism. Denial. Even despair. As a biologist, if I were observing a particular organism or population, I'd look at the behavior. And I'd see certain behaviors as a response to a survival threat. Maladaptive, in some cases. Such as the group behavioral response to global warming. The response, so far, is maladaptive. It won't prolong survival."

"So the culture's like a prey animal. In its death throes."

"Well, I mean, the animal *does* escape, sometimes. Occasionally the TI strategy works."

"But it *won't* work. In this case."

"Yeah, no. This is a fight-or-flight situation. With the climate. And there's no possibility of flight."

Anne pushed her eggs around on her plate.

"They're too wet. Aren't they."

"Kind of."

"I'll eat them. You want a slice of sourdough?"

In her practice she'd offer up coping techniques. When other interventions weren't called for or agreed to. Rituals of self-care. Open the window. Take deep breaths. Put on music.

But lately she'd lie in bed, unable to fall asleep, thinking of crowds. The patients in their great ranks, like a sad army.

Clients, she was supposed to call them, but she preferred the word *patient*. Always had. It wasn't that she wanted to position herself as an MD. More that *client* sounded transactional. Applied to tax-preparation customers and real-estate buyers alike.

While *patient* was a good word. Since it also meant forbearing. Forgiving, even. Therapy took time.

She saw them in hospital gowns, staring toward the horizon. The patients everywhere. In institutions and outside them.

Maladaptive.

Because if you multiplied that prescription, for acceptance and accommodation, and made it into policy, you'd have systemic failure. On the macro level, acceptance of the normal would mean death.

It had started to seem to her that, as she counseled her patients on how to live better within that new normal—or the abnormality that passed for normal—she was delivering therapeutic euthanasia.

With her head on the pillow, feeling the warm air sweep over her skin as it moved the curtains, she pictured herself walking along the rows of patients. Who stood watching and waiting and never moved. Dosing each one with a sedative and a painkiller.

Palliative care.

Stephanie tried to make her feel better.

"You know the drill," she said as they lay there. "Your job isn't about systems. It's about individuals. Helping them know what they can control and what they can't."

"But it isn't just *my* job. It's everyone's job. Is how it feels to me these days. Everyone's going around saying, Feel better. And here's how to do it. Surrender your agency. Be at peace with catastrophe."

"Listen," said Stephanie, swiveling onto an elbow. Propping her head on her hand. "Do you have any idea where this is coming from? I only ask because historically, when you've been distressed like this, it's usually been transferred to you by a patient. Where your clinical detachment has partially failed. No offense meant."

Anne shook her head. "It's ambient. It's obvious."

But after Stephanie turned onto her other side and started snoring, she went back over her patient interactions. There *was* someone. A kid. Well, a young man. His bleakness was persuasive. The fear, he said, was common sense.

It *shouldn't* be healed, he argued. It *shouldn't* be erased.

The compulsion to normalize, he said, was the real pathology. Being enacted on a grand scale. A sociopolitical scale.

She'd sent him to Stegman for an SSRI.

In their last session he'd told her about a dinner he'd been to at his girlfriend's house where one of the other guests seemed to be made of plastic.

Uh-oh, she'd thought. For a second her association was Capgras. Impostor syndrome. She'd had an elderly patient who believed her husband had been replaced by a copy. And the copy was a murderous android.

Janet, had been the patient's name. Sweet woman. Far too eager to please.

She wondered if Janet was still alive. It had been years.

Here, though, it turned out to be a metaphor.

"And the thing is, I used to have a crush on his girlfriend," he said. "Back in high school. She's the older sister of my girlfriend now. Smart and attractive. But, so, maybe you're thinking, I had a vested interest in not liking the guy. Territorial. But it *wasn't* that. He just, all he could do, in the conversation, was recycle these stale talking points. These pieces of pat received wisdom from business school. He has this smug certainty that all the systems will keep functioning. Systems of wealth and power. The way they always have."

"Maybe they will. And that was what threatened you."

He was silent. In the Zoom window, she watched him pick up a thermos and drink from it. Hoped it was water.

When he set it down he nodded. "It does threaten me. But it also threatens you. It threatens us all. And everyone after."

"When you say *it*," she said, "what does that mean?"

"The complacency. The pretense. That all this climate and mass extinction shit isn't a five-alarm emergency. That what we need isn't a worldwide revolution. Yesterday."

She sat with that a minute. Her turn to be silent.

"Let's get back to this guest. Your feelings about him."

"Sure. Let's get back to talking about a dinner party."

"You were the one who brought it up. Isn't there more to unpack there?"

"This is what I'm referring to. The dinner's trivial. My feelings about it are *trivial*. They just don't matter, Anne."

"So everything has to be about the need for a revolution?"

"There you go! Unpacked! That's what I'm saying. Everything, everything, everything. Should be about that. From now till 2050. And beyond."

"OK, then. If that's how you feel, why are you spending your time working at a bar? Helping your customers self-medicate?"

"Uh . . . because I need a job? And I'm no one?"

"You're no one?"

He sat back in his chair. Threw up his hands.

"You know what I mean."

"But you're *not* no one."

"I am. And, sorry, so are you."

"You're saying we're similarly powerless."

"You've got a career and I don't have anything, but we both listen to people complain all day. And we both drug them, too."

Behind him was a poster of a pretty actress wearing a vest that looked like armor. Her long hair flowed around her wildly. Like Medusa's snakes.

She felt like saying, It's hard to take you seriously. With Xena the Warrior Princess in the background. Or whoever.

She didn't say it, of course.

Anyway, they'd already gone over fifty minutes.

Radicalized. That was another term she heard all the time that she didn't remember hearing so much when she was younger. It had been used in the sixties—mostly around Vietnam protesters, if she recalled right from her reading, and maybe Malcolm X—but then it seemed to recede until 9/11. When it turned into a radio and TV staple.

And it was never a positive. Back in the Vietnam era, you could be a radical for peace. Or justice. Now a radical was only a terrorist. It was Al Qaeda, the Taliban, the white supremacists who stormed the Capitol. The violent extremists.

She read practitioners who specialized in radicalization. There were networks. Radicalized youth were spread across the demographic spectrum, rich and poor, single and in relationships.

But neglect, psychological abuse, and abandonment were strong predictors.

On those fronts Nick was a piss-poor candidate, in her opinion.

Still. You never knew. A worldwide revolution, he had said.

Red flag? Or standard existential angst?

He wasn't talking about taking up arms. No history of violence. No suicidal ideation, as far as she knew. He wasn't socially isolated. But then again, it often seemed to come out of nowhere.

"I'm not sure how to help him," she said to Stegman on the phone.

They were both in their kitchens. Making dinner.

"Sounds like you're pretty enmeshed," said Stegman. She could hear the pop of his bourbon cork. For a neuropsychiatrist, he had some old-school vices. "In his rationalizations."

"I guess so."

"When in doubt, take a step back. Go to trauma and repression. Have you spent enough time on ECD?"

"His childhood was uneventful. Is how it sounded to me."

"Impossible."

She heard cracking—a tray of ice cubes being twisted, that was it. And then the glug-glug-glug of him pouring the whiskey.

"Come on, Lou. Can we get real? *Relatively*. Stable, protected, no upheavals. He's got married parents who've lived in the same upper-middle-class neighborhood for more than twenty years. He was never bullied, molested, or sidelined by his peers. First sexual experience at age sixteen. No issues of gender or sexual identity. Academically, and in sports, some moderate successes with a few minor failures. A decent balance for resiliency. He does some pot. That's it."

"Don't be reductive. Dig deeper."

He sipped.

His earbuds captured ambient sound too well.

Nick wasn't resistant to talking about his childhood—he enjoyed it. Got caught up in the narratives. A bike he once had with a banana seat. It had been his father's before it was his. In the seventies. A cousin teaching him to ski at Big Bear, all expert and condescending, then falling flat on his face. His little sister hiding his underwear. When the school bus was already moving along their block. His mom giving him bowl cuts in fifth grade because he refused to go to the barber. Didn't like how it smelled in there.

The barber had halitosis.

"No repressed trauma," he said near the end of a session. "Except for, maybe, that barber. Man. Someone should have told him. His breath was a biohazard. And that was *way* before COVID."

"You were a golden boy."

He smiled. "No. I just had a golden life."

"But, somehow, you're not a golden man."

The smile vanished.

"The guy at the dinner, say. Is that what a golden man looks like?"

He made a grunt of irritation. "I wish I'd never mentioned it."

"But you did. There must have been a reason."

"Sure, yeah. In the eyes of MAGA voters who refused to wear a face mask or get vaccinated, and vote against solar and wind, that man would probably look golden."

"What about your parents? Who gave you that golden childhood and sent you to a golden university? Would he seem golden to them?"

He sighed. "I doubt it. They're registered Democrats."

"So what would golden look like for them?"

He cocked his head. Fiddled with a pen. "Maybe Luis. My brother-in-law. He's DACA and studying to be an immigration lawyer. From a Guatemalan family who were refugees but never got citizenship. His father's a farmworker in the Central Valley. Probably has off-the-charts chemical exposure. His mother works at a bakery. Luis is a good guy. He's, like, pursuing the American dream."

"But you're not pursuing that dream. You used to be, but you're not anymore. So your parents are disappointed in you."

The poster of the warrior princess, she noticed, had been taken down. Either that or he was Zooming in from a different room.

"I *had* the dream," he said quietly. "Then I woke up."

"And now you can't remember it."

"Not true. I remember it perfectly."

"But it doesn't motivate you anymore."

"Anne. It was never real life. It was only a dream."

His monologues had a youthful poignance. They stayed with her for their earnestness.

A dream gets implanted in you, he'd told her in an early session. A dream of the heroic individual, tall and powerful as a god. The monomyth! A dream of infinite selfishness. But instead of liberating you, it binds you to the wheel. The great wheel moves the plow. And the plow tills the field.

"And far away," he said, "always ahead of you but never reached, there's a shimmering mirage. That they call happiness."

She agreed to go on a field trip. Over a weekend. It wasn't Stephanie's own study but the project of a new colleague that she'd been invited to observe. Had to do with insects and the waterbirds that ate them.

"We could do a hike, right?" said Stephanie. "It's been a while."

"A hike-hike?" asked Anne. "One of those death marches that call for trekking poles and a heavy pack? Or a pleasant, relaxing walk? With an elevation gain under a thousand feet?"

"Huh. I wonder what your vote is?"

"I'm not in the mood for a death march."

"It's a wetland. Like elevation gain is maybe two feet."

"But with mosquitoes."

"I hope so. No mosquitoes would be a bad sign. For the study."

"And we're not allowed DEET. Because it's so toxic."

"Correct."

So they drove out of the city. Across the state line, into Nevada. It was a rare kind of wetland they were headed to, said Stephanie: a wetland in the desert. Shrinking every year.

Along the freeway they drove, past car dealerships and outlet malls and onto smaller roads. They passed a ranch flying a Trump flag almost as big as the farmhouse itself.

"Are you supposed to have a flag with, like, a person's name on it?" she asked Stephanie.

"You're the shrink," said Stephanie. "You tell me."

On the barn was painted AMERICA FIRST. Just to be clear.

A few miles on they picked out another sign, tiny and barely visible in a brushy patch of wildflowers. BLACK LIVES MATTER. On a rainbow background faded by the sun.

"In the war of the signs, I guess we know who's winning," said Stephanie.

They stopped at a modest, low building, the refuge headquarters. Stephanie talked to a ranger while Anne used the restroom. She didn't like to pee behind bushes.

For Stephanie it was an occupational hazard. Not for her. She'd picked a job with flush toilets.

"He was wearing a hat like Smokey the Bear's," she said as they got back into the car.

It made her think of a bygone era, when the park rangers were everyone's friends. And no outlaw ranchers faced them down with armed militias.

"Smokey was a real bear," said Stephanie. "Did you know that? There's a museum to him. Next to his grave. Near Lincoln National Forest. I went there once on a road trip."

"I thought he was invented in World War II," said Anne. "So people wouldn't leave their campfires burning and destroy the lumber supply."

"Yeah but a few years later they found a baby bear in a tree. Badly burned from a fire. They called him Hotfoot first but then changed his name to Smokey and sent him to live at a zoo in DC. With Ham the space chimp. When he died they sent the body back to New Mexico. To be buried in his old forest home."

"Sweet."

"There was another Smokey after him. Smokey II. But he wasn't as popular. When *he* died they burned him."

After a while on a bumpy dirt road they came to a place where the road got wet. Reeds all around them, rustling and scraping against the car when the road was narrow. She heard mud spattering into the car's wheel wells.

"He said we'd see the survey flags."

"Like, Day-Glo pink?"

"You see one? OK. Look for a pullout on the left."

A Jeep was parked. And a pickup truck.

A woman in waders and an orange vest approached as they were getting out their hats and water bottles. "Steph! Hi! You found us!"

They started discussing the fieldwork. Something with plots and water samples.

"Inverts," the colleague kept saying.

Association: Krafft-Ebing. The sexologists who used to call gay
people inverts. Gay men had a feminine soul in a man's body,
they had suggested. Lesbians had the reverse.

But the colleague was referring to invertebrates.

"It's looking grim," she told Stephanie. "The densities are even
lower than we expected."

Drought was a factor. Water withdrawals from the nearby
river. But pesticide-spraying was also a likely culprit.

"They spray pesticides? On a wildlife refuge?" asked Anne.

"Oh, absolutely," said the colleague. "To subsidize the farmers."

Stephanie'd forgotten to introduce them. She wasn't always on
top of the niceties.

The colleague offered to take them both into the swampy
water—she'd brought some extra pairs of waders—but Anne
demurred.

"I'll just go look around with her a bit," said Stephanie. "Maybe
for half an hour. We can do the hike after. OK?"

"If you stand in the bed of the truck, you'll be able to see us," said
the colleague. "There's a cooler with water and beer. And lemonade."

"I'm Anne, by the way," said Anne.

"Nice to meet you," said the colleague.

Still no name.

Task-oriented. And far more interested in arthropods than
people. Stephanie was an outlier in her department—focused on
the big picture. Commonalities among lifeforms. Most of the rest
of them saw the world through smaller windows. Shied away from
anything they thought might be viewed as anthropomorphic.

We were us, to the biologists, and the others were the others.

Not so different from shrinks, actually.

But the colleague was considerate. She set up a folding chair for Anne in the pickup bed. The ground was too muddy, she explained. Its legs would sink in. She spun it over the tailgate one-handed, then flicked her wrist to open it. Deft.

Stephanie pulled on the waders and a vest and the two of them went forging off into the reeds. Anne popped the tab on a beer and tried sitting in the chair. But sitting down, she couldn't see anything but the pale-green grasses.

So she perched on the cab of the truck instead. Cross-legged and sipping. Looked for the high-vis vests and made out five of them.

They were counting insects. And she was counting people.

They bent over, moving forward a few shuffles at a time. The work was painstaking. Slow and painstaking. Someone wearing a bug net over his face, not too far from the truck, lifted a container of yellowish water up to the light.

When there was a light breeze, it was pleasant up there on the truck cab. A sea of grasses waving before her. Here and there, a stretch of glittering water.

Far above, sometimes a plane.

But when it was still it was stifling. She almost felt claustrophobic. Though surrounded by air.

Mosquitoes began to descend. She slapped at them. Mosquitoes had always been drawn to her. Stephanie they ignored.

She wished Stephanie would come back.

The longer she waited, the more she thought about her patients. Still Nick, but also Brent and Helen. All three of them preoccupied by the looming state of emergency.

If they were here, would they be comforted by the sight of those orange vests? Moving through the muddy water, dedicated to the granular detail of insects? Performing their careful measurements?

Maybe Helen. She believed in science and hope. Local solutions. Resistance.

But not Brent. Brent was a hardened cynic when it came to his fellow humans. On the spectrum, plus OCD. He said the summer sea ice in the Arctic was already a ghost. A foregone conclusion. Only a handful of years more. And as went the Arctic, he said—bobbing his head in a constant rhythm—so went Greenland. When Greenland melted, he told her, that would be about 23 feet right there. Sea-level wise. And it was melting fast. Faster than previous projections. So, there went the coastal cities. Antarctica would lag, but still melt too. On down the road.

230 feet, he said. When all the ice was gone.

He had no children. Would never have any.

A sound decision, certainly. Though not a sociopath, he exhibited low empathy. To him the future was of little personal interest. It was a problem for others to deal with.

He *did* regret how it would end up for the animals. And the plants and trees. He had a soft spot for those who didn't speak and kept a spreadsheet of confirmed extinctions. Sometimes he'd use up a whole session discussing a tree frog or a butterfly. The last attested sightings. The animals' natural history.

During a frenzied OCD episode, he'd text her dozens of pictures of Hawaiian snails. Or mussels in Appalachia.

Rest in peace, brothers and sisters, he would text.

RIP. RIP. RIP. RIP. RIP.

She'd noticed clouds but hadn't paid much attention. The forecast had said cloudy, but no rain. By the time it started she'd been reduced to propping her sunglasses on top of her head and playing a game on her phone. No signal, so she couldn't read the news.

The game was so basic Stephanie made fun of her for playing it.

"Mindless," Stephanie would say.

"Exactly. It's a form of meditation," she'd claim.

You sorted panels of color into vials. That was it. She was on level 1,228.

Recently, she reflected, Nick's affect had shifted for the better. Partly the Lexapro, no doubt, but also the girlfriend. She situated him in his life. It was a good match—the bond was surprisingly strong.

To her, he *was* golden.

Anne's guess was he would go, eventually, the way most upper-middle-class people went. Toward the domestic. Ensconce himself in a smaller world he could control.

Maybe he'd stay on the Lexapro long-term. It was possible.

And go forward, like so many, with despair held at bay by comfort. Nestled in affection.

The first drop she saw was on the screen. Then, rapidly, rain was beating down on the truck. Hollow, tinny pings on the metal. Far off, a spidery bolt of lightning.

She gazed out over the sea of reeds. Were the biologists coming in? Or would they keep on working?

She saw the orange vests draw closer to each other. She couldn't tell which one was Stephanie. Faintly, she heard their voices.

She thought of signaling to them. Waving her arms.

But what would she be signaling? It's raining? And I'm here?

Stephanie already knew these things.

With the lightning, she should get down from the truck. The bed was slick with water.

She picked her way across it, folded the camp chair and propped it on its side, and stepped over the tailgate. Down into the slippery mud.

Oh! But the car was locked. The keys were in Stephanie's pocket. No reason to lock it, out here, but the car locked itself if you left it unattended.

"Dammit," she said.

The rain was coming harder. She was getting soaked.

She leaned against the side of the car, folding her arms. Her fault, too. She could have asked for the keys. It hadn't occurred to her.

Her clothes were sodden and her hair was plastered to her scalp, dripping down her face and onto her shoulders. She wiped a tickling drip off the back of her neck.

Around her the rain made a vast pattering sound in the reeds. So many small sounds she couldn't track them.

So you're wet, she told herself. Big deal. That's done. At some point, you'll be dry again. Just listen, why don't you.

The sounds went on and on. Spread about her in their inseparable millions. A symphony of water and plants. If she listened without resistance, the sounds would take her beyond the shivering.

Beyond the inconvenience. Into the elemental.

It was hard to believe the elements would fail us, she thought.

Less hard to believe we would fail them.

All around, all around, all around.

The rain is coming down, she said to herself.

She raised her face and closed her eyes.

Let me be liquid. Bathed in the clouds.

Right now, here in the home that made us, we still have the rain.

COSMETOLOGIST

"I still want a triangle in the front," said the guest. "I feel like the full Brazilian would make me look like I'm trying to pass as a prepubescent. You know?"

"I get it," Fia told her. "So leave the natural growth? Or do you want me to shape it a bit? Kind of a neater triangle?"

"I mean, the problem with shaping it is, I have to tweeze the edges between waxings. The stray hairs drive me crazy. You can get obsessive with the tweezing. You know?"

"I do," she said, nodding. "Tweezing's addictive."

"Just sitting on the toilet. Looking down there and tweezing, tweezing, tweezing. Hurts my neck."

"OK. Just natural in front. Can you go ahead and butterfly your legs for me?"

She couldn't remember why they were supposed to say butterfly. Maybe so it sounded pretty. Really it was a diamond: the knees went out, but the feet stayed close to each other. So from crotch to ankles, the shape was a diamond. And diamonds were also pretty.

Sometimes she did say diamond, but guests understood butterfly better. The act of dropping their knees outward was like a butterfly opening its wings.

It was the movement, not the shape.

She twirled the wax on the stick. That was about movement too. Twirl, twirl, twirl. When she started her fingers had been stiff after every shift. It couldn't be so hot it burned, but it also couldn't cool.

"Is the temperature OK?" she asked, spreading the wax on an inner thigh.

"Fine, fine," said the guest. She'd taken her socks off—some did and some didn't—and her toenails had roses on them.

"I like your nails," said Fia.

With the bikinis and Brazilians you had to keep the conversation flowing. If you went quiet, the guests felt self-conscious. It hit them, in the silence, that they'd strolled in off the street, spread their legs under fluorescent lights, and didn't know you from Adam.

But there you were, touching their private parts.

"You do? I asked for daisies, but she did roses. There's always a language barrier. At nail salons."

"*Tell* me about it."

"They nod and act like they understand, but then do something different. And at that point you're too shy to stop them. You don't want to be high maintenance."

"I know. You're kind of like, whatever."

"You surrender."

"You raise the white flag."

"Although not everyone is shy. There was this lady right next to me, a couple of pedicures ago, who made them change the color. After both feet were done. And it was gel. Did she *pay* double? I doubt it."

"So this is the first labia. This one could hurt a bit. Since it's been over six weeks. Breathe out. OK? Now, one, two, three."

She ripped it off. A sharp intake of breath.

"Oh! But that wasn't so bad . . . I have a friend who tried to do it at home. Her Brazilian."

"Oh, wow! Really?"

"In the early lockdown. I told her it was crazy. She literally ripped some skin off. Her vagina."

Her vulva, actually. But who was arguing?

"It's tough. I *never* do my own. And I have training."

"Plus the wax itself. It's so much better here. Than those home kits from the drugstore."

"Well, yeah. Our wax, and I'm not saying this just because I work here, is hands down the best. It's a proprietary formula."

God's truth. The wax was awesome.

"She said her husband wouldn't go down on her if she had hair there. Or even stubble."

You rolled with the punches. Kept the talk ball rolling.

"I mean, that's kind of sad? I guess? Like, as a waxer I'm biased, but there shouldn't be *conditions*. Right?"

"Exactly. I was like, I'm not a huge feminist or anything, but shit, girl. Know your rights."

"Seriously. OK, take a deep breath again and let it out."

"No one wants pubes in their teeth. But sometimes, like in a global pandemic, it's just the cost of doing business."

"We all made sacrifices."

The guest laughed.

But after she said *sacrifices*, Fia thought of Tomás. Who had died. Her aunt, rocking back and forth and crying.

One day he was riding his bike with training wheels, the next day he couldn't breathe.

She had to shake it off.

"Are we done there?" said the guest.

"All done. I just need to get the rear. You can flip or you can hold your knees up to your face for me. Whatever's better."

"I'll hold them up. I don't like the doggy-style thing."

"I know what you mean."

"But you've been great. It hardly even hurt."

"Have a gorgeous day," she said to the guest when she walked her to the lobby to pay.

The receptionists were always supposed to say it, but after she got the tip envelope, Tamra went right back to staring at her phone. She said it was a dumb expression. Plus she was Goth and it didn't match her style.

And it *was* dumb, but Fia said it anyway. Since Tamra refused. She said it maybe ten times a shift, making up for Tamra's sullen silence. Have a gorgeous day! Gorgeous day! Gorgeous day!

Some nights it echoed in her head.

Eight minutes till the next appointment. She'd thought maybe they'd let them slow down, with not as many guests coming in, but instead they'd just fired the newer staff and kept the schedules tight. For the waxers who were left.

So she went to the bathroom. If she didn't, Pattie would sidle in from her own room and talk to her the whole time. She scrolled back to the photos on her phone. Tomás's grave, with a vase of roses on it. It must have been the roses on the toenails that had reminded her of him.

A tiny toy bike was at the grave too. Blue, the same color as his real one. He'd loved the blue bike. He'd gotten it that Christmas, the Christmas of 2019, and rode around all the time. Put stickers on it of Pokémon characters. Mostly the cute yellow one.

He'd told Fia, "They say he's not a pika. Even though his name is Pikachu. But I like pikas. They live on mountains and squeak."

He hadn't been big or anything. He just had asthma. That was it. Lots of kids in his neighborhood had asthma. It was near a huge trucking depot. And none of those other kids had died from the COVID.

The doctor had said, "I'm afraid we can't explain his susceptibility. It's unusual, statistically, but we *are* seeing a few of these cases. I wish we'd been able to do more for him."

Since then her aunt was a shut-in. She used to go salsa dancing once a week. And love her job as a dental hygienist. Now she watched TV all day. It had been years, but no one could get her to stop watching TV. Horse races, mostly.

She never even *liked* horses before. Now she said she wanted to watch them running. Around and around in circles.

"They say the horses know it when they win," she'd told Fia once. As Fia sat beside her on the couch that smelled like a dirty bed. "So it's supposed to be fun for them. But I don't believe it. I see their eyes. What the horse thinks is, I run and I run. But I can never get away."

Shit. Two minutes over. And she hadn't wiped down the table yet. She blew her nose and washed her hands.

The next guest was legs and underarms. At first Fia didn't recognize her under the mask. Corporate had said it was up to them. Whatever the staff was comfortable with. At their location. And they decided, masks. Back then.

Tamra wasn't into it, but she got outvoted. So she'd kept her mask under her chin. Useless.

Fia stopped liking her, then.

That had been ages ago, but other than Tamra most of them still wore masks. Most days.

The guests, not so much.

"It's been a while," said Fia. "Great to see you!"

"What can I say, there wasn't anyone to impress," said the guest. A middle-aged professor. She was a good tipper and friendly. "But tomorrow I've got a date."

"Oh, wow," said Fia. "I remember those." Twirl, twirl.

Trudy, that was her name. It said Gertrude on her birth certificate, she'd told Fia before. But who would ever go by Gertrude? Only Gertrude Stein could pull it off.

Trudy was in her fifties. They had their own celebrities.

"Probably won't end well," she said. "I found him on an app. But it's an excuse to get out of the house. And wear a skirt for once."

"I used a couple of apps. It's how I met my boyfriend."

"Really? That's reassuring! It was my kid who convinced me to do it. He thinks I'm antisocial. Says it's unhealthy. So I'm going for dinner with some random guy to make my son happy."

"That's adorable! How old is your son again?"

"Almost fifteen."

"It's nice that he cares. My brother, when he was that age, he didn't even notice our mother was a human being. He saw her as, just like, his personal chef and housecleaner."

"Well. I'm terrible at both those things. So my advice to mothers is, avoid them. Then there won't be any confusion."

Fia laughed.

"Anyway, the guy I'm going on a date with claims to own a food-service business. So maybe the food will be good, at least."

"Oh, nice," said Fia.

"But it could easily be one of those deals where you show up and he's twenty years older than he said he was. Which in this case would be pushing seventy. And has no hair at all. Except in his ears and nose."

"Though bald guys, some of them are cute. Don't you think?"

"Sure. If they don't try to hide it. With combovers. Or plugs."

"What about hair transplants? Like Elon Musk?"

"Elon Musk got a hair transplant?"

"It's obvious! OK, raise your other arm for me."

"So I'm picturing it, right now, like when someone gets an organ transplant. And they fly the organ to the hospital roof in a helicopter with the red cross on it. In a small cooler. And inside the cooler is Elon Musk's new hair. On ice."

"Like a little brown squirrel."

"But I guess it'd have to be attached to a scalp."

"No way!"

"But wait. Are plugs the same as implants?"

"I think the new implants are better. The surgeons do, like, individual follicles. I'm getting my cosmetology license and they talked about it once. It can run a guy, like, fifteen grand. Or more."

"That's pennies to Elon."

"He could probably afford the whole-scalp option."

"He could afford a scalp on the black market."

"Do you want me to do your toes? No extra charge. And it's really quick."

"Thank you. Those toe hairs are ugly."

"You don't have too many. I had a guest once whose toes looked like they had miniature beards."

"That could come in handy! If you painted eyes and a mouth on the toenails, you could do puppet shows."

And there he was again. Tomás.

He used to do puppet shows for her. With sock puppets. One had been a dinosaur, the other a chicken. He'd glued googly eyes on them. Made them talk in different voices. The dinosaur said funny, smart things and the chicken only said boc-boc. And pecked him.

"Sofía. Hey. Are you OK?"

"Yeah, no, I . . ."

"You want to stop for a minute? I can wait. Take all the time you need. There's no hurry."

Trudy swung her legs off the table. The toes had wax on them. Dark-blue blobs. She reached past to the Kleenex box on the counter. Pulled one out and handed it to Fia.

Touched her forearm. Clasping it lightly.

"I used to have this little cousin," said Fia, dabbing. Her mascara could be running. "He made his own puppets."

"He did?"

"There was a dinosaur. With . . . with teeth made of white felt."

"OK."

"He said it was a nice dinosaur. Not a mean one. It had big teeth. But it was still a plant-eater. He said. And its enemy . . . its enemy was a chicken."

"Hey, sure. Man. Chickens can be scary. They'll peck each other half to death. If you let them. Plus, little-known fact, their eggs and their shit come out of the exact same hole."

Fia hiccupped. Half laughing.

You were *so* not supposed to let stuff like this happen. Ever.

"I'm sorry. I'm so sorry."

"You don't have to apologize to me. Sometimes things just hit us. When it's not convenient. I'm fine with it."

"So he, Tomás, he passed away. In 2020. From the COVID. He was only nine."

"Oh, *no.*"

"He was, he seemed so healthy. Except for, he had asthma. An inhaler. But he skated. He played basketball. He was fit."

"I'm so sorry."

"And since then my aunt, she doesn't want to live anymore. She says she can't kill herself. Because she has two other children. And they need her. But she can't stand to go on living. Even five years later. She thinks about him all the time. She said it to my mom."

"I'd feel that way too. For a while. I truly would."

"He wasn't even—he wasn't even mine. I mean, he was my little guy. My favorite cousin. But still, not my own *kid*. And sometimes I remember. It was just the anniversary last week. Of him passing. And it came rushing . . . and then it's like, how could I ever have a baby myself? If that can happen?"

"I know. Believe me. It's the worst thing in the world."

"I don't want to."

"And you don't have to, either."

"I just don't *want* to."

"And that's OK."

She hadn't known it. Before this. And now it was here.

Her whole extended family had tons of kids. It was practically your job. Once you had kids, you were in the club. For good.

But she couldn't do it. Ever.

She couldn't stand the thought.

"They can be taken away," she said. Swiveled her shoulders and pulled out another tissue. "Nine years. And then . . . overnight."

"It can happen. People don't really think of that, when they get pregnant. They have to ignore it. The possibility of tragedy. But no one says you have to be one of them."

It took her a minute to get her eyes cleaned up. Above the

mask. Looking into a small mirror she kept in a drawer. Trudy was quiet, waiting.

She was so embarrassed.

"Don't worry about me," said Trudy. "OK? Please."

"No, but, thank you. I still have to take the wax off. Of your toes."

"All right, yes. I won't say no. Or else they'll stick to my shoes. I'll be going to my date in those filthy old sneakers. And if it goes really well, in a surprising turn of events, I won't be able to take them off. I'll be all, Sorry, no, I *always* keep these sneakers on. It's just my thing."

Fia laughed a bit.

She was still sniffly.

Trudy wiggled her toes. "Uh-oh," she said, peering at the toe wax. "It's gotten so hard. Will it still work?"

"I'll get it. I promise. These toes are going to look as smooth as the day they were born."

Trudy gave her the tip right in the room. Instead of waiting for Tamra to hand her the little envelope in reception.

Before they went into the hall, she turned to Fia and opened her arms for a hug.

"I'm fully vaccinated, of course," she said. "All the boosters."

"Me too."

At the register Fia handed over the slip. "Four to six weeks out. For the next appointment," she told Tamra.

"Thank you so much," said Trudy.

"No, thank *you*," she said. "I really mean it."

Didn't even say gorgeous day.

But after Trudy disappeared into the parking lot she stood by herself at the glass storefront, gazing out.

Cars glittered like ugly jewels.

OPTIMIST

Since he couldn't run distance anymore, Buzz had been looking for new hobbies. Though he didn't call them that.

There were some early misfires. She tried to be supportive. First it was learning to sea kayak. Which wasn't so easy, living an hour from the beach in light traffic. An hour and a half if there was a slowdown on the 10. He bought a starter boat and took lessons.

But when the lesson package was used up he said kayaking made his back ache. He hadn't mastered the rollover. Tended to panic. And feel like he was drowning.

Next it was welding. But that lasted two weeks.

Then he decided to take up disaster preparedness. Ordered a lot of supplies. Water filtration devices. Dried-out astronaut food. Solar flashlights. Silver blankets that stopped you from getting hypothermia. If you were alone in the nonexistent forest. She'd been like, Buzz. What are we going to need those for? You think we'll head up to Lake Tahoe, in a disaster, and then start freezing there?

He cut back the limbs on a few trees that were near the house. In case of a fire that might come tearing in from the canyon. He didn't have a chainsaw, he said, but he could use his good old Sawzall.

She watched from the back porch, nursing a margarita. Afraid he'd saw off his arm. Kept her phone on the table to call 911.

But the expensive, high-tech power storage unit that went up on the wall—that one did him in. After he failed to hook it up right and had to call in an electrician, who openly belittled his efforts, he decided they were sufficiently prepared.

The joint problems that stopped him from running had coincided with their empty nest. Liza off at college, with their new son-in-law in tow, and then Nick moving out. Into a studio near the bar where he worked.

Buzz had been pushing him to move out for months—he should stand on his own two feet, Buzz had said again and again, at the age of twenty-three—but once the decision was finally made, he backpedaled.

"I've been thinking," he said. "Why should you take on that extra overhead? Rents are crazy right now. And we've got plenty of room."

"I gotta go, Dad," said Nick. Patted him on the back. "The rough beast slouches towards Bethlehem. Its hour come round at last."

She'd found Buzz, on a few occasions, standing in Nick's empty bedroom. Looking around like he was seeing it for the first time.

"What are we going to do with all the space?" he'd ask when she came in.

He started hinting that they should have a family project. Take in some refugees from Afghanistan.

"You don't mean it," she said. "That's a huge commitment!"

"But why not?" he asked. "We *can!*"

"If we had a guesthouse, maybe," she said. "But as it is now, our privacy would be gone. Buzz. Picture yourself coming downstairs for breakfast. You haven't had your coffee and you're wearing your boxer briefs. Let's say you tied one on the night before. Watching a race and downing too many beers. The knee's bothering you. Or the hip. And there, sitting at the dining room table, is a whole family of Afghans."

He shrugged. "It wouldn't be so bad."

"Maybe they're all wearing hoods. And have those piercing green eyes. Like the girl from the famous magazine cover. In the eighties."

"We could just take on a single Afghan. A bachelor."

"I don't even want a bachelor. Just sitting there? At the table? Expecting a hot breakfast? I don't know if you noticed, but I just got done with serving two *other* people. For almost a quarter-century. I.e., our *children*. So I could really use a break."

"He could make his own meals. Couldn't he?"

"Well, we don't have a guesthouse. So."

Unfortunately, he took her objection and ran with it. What if they *did* have a guesthouse?

He showed her pictures online. You could buy prefab sheds. Tiny houses, hip and modern. The colors could match the main house. Hell, for eighty grand they'd even finish it for you. It could have a solar water heater. And a kitchenette.

"Buzz. Do we have an extra eighty grand? Burning a hole in our pocket?"

"I think we could swing it. We have those ETFs."

"But it's a terrible time to sell. We'll have to pay capital gains, won't we? And the ETFs are for our retirement."

He grumbled a bit, so she thought he was letting it go.

But a few days later he brought it up again.

"They even handle the permits for you," he said. "The tiny-house companies. They do it all. You hire a local company to pour the slab, and bingo. They bring in the tiny house and set it up on the slab."

He measured parts of the backyard and the driveway. Marked lines in chalk using a brand-new laser level and blue string.

"See? They could back the truck in right here. Maybe one bush we'd have to lose. And the Japanese maple. But we can relocate it."

"Buzz, listen," she said in bed. "I feel like you're rushing into this. Three months ago, you were all about sea kayaking. And where's the sea kayak now? In the garage. With spiderwebs on it the size of a housecat."

"This is different," he said. "The refugees can't wait."

"But eighty thousand dollars, Buzz. And we're paying Liza's tuition. And their rent."

"It's an investment, Amy. There's a housing shortage in this state. It'll pay for itself. If we ever sell this place."

If she said yes, maybe he'd forget about it. Maybe the refugees would be like the sea kayak.

And there were worse things than having a guesthouse. Liza and Luis could stay there in the summers, say. If Luis got time off. And they wanted a space of their own.

Plus Buzz might have a point, about the added value.

So she gave in.

There was a waitlist for the tiny houses, which she figured would give her some breathing room.

But he was impatient. Got on the phone. It was for refugees, he told the woman at the tiny-house company.

"These people are coming from a war-torn country. Where girls can't go to school. And the Taliban might show up at your door and take away your ninety-year-old father. Or ISIS-K might blow you up. They need a home ASAP. Isn't there anything you can do?"

It was an outfit up in Fresno. Progressives on a mission to bring their tiny houses to the masses.

"OK. We'll do our best to fit you in," the woman said.

Then the slab was poured. And two weeks later, there was the tiny house. With tradespeople working on it. Plumbers. Painters. More electricians.

Buzz ordered appliances. And furniture.

"I think there's room for a family of three," he told her. "The couple can sleep on the sofa bed, right? It's a queen. And we can get a folding cot for the kid. Store it right there in the closet. See, it doesn't have to be just a bachelor. They can make their own meals."

"They'll feel so crowded, though. I mean, how long will it be?"

"Depends on the bureaucracy. Hell, some of them are living on military bases. Holloman AFB and Fort Bliss. Some are still over there. Or in Qatar. Waiting for SIVs."

She'd meant how long would they *live* there. Not when would they come. But anyway.

"SIVs?"

"Special immigration visas."

"I think two people would be better than three," she said. "In a tiny house."

Ideally two, but three in a pinch, was what they decided. He put their names on a list. Made phone calls and sent emails. Resettlement agencies. Local groups. A politician or two.

Late at night, in bed, he'd watch footage from camps. Interviews. Lists of new bad things the Taliban was doing.

Even at work he made calls. He'd get home and tell her about meetings he'd missed. On hold with some agency or another.

Meanwhile he was stress-eating. It used to be all high-fiber bread and beans and vegetables, when he was training for a race.

And he'd always been training for a race.

Now it was bags of potato chips. He'd eat them right out of the bag and leave the empties on the counter. With crumbs in the bottom. Once the teenagers were out of the house, he'd decided to act like one.

His midsection was getting thick.

She didn't want to make him feel bad, but it wasn't great. Before, she'd always admired his physique. These days she'd see him coming out of the shower with a towel around his waist and think, Who's that middle-aged schlub in my bedroom? With the flabby love handles?

He didn't seem to notice.

"Do you think maybe you're getting a little obsessive?" she asked.

"Sure," he said. "I'm driving fast, Amy. I have to. My eyes are on the horizon."

"I don't remember you being so passionate. About the refugee crisis."

"This is a special case. We abandoned a whole nation! People who cooperated. Risked their lives because they trusted us. And now there are Ukrainians, too. And the Afghans are forgotten. It's our sovereign duty."

The wheels of state weren't turning fast enough, Buzz said.

He occupied himself rearranging the furniture in the tiny house. Hanging topical art in it, such as photos of Afghan nature. Basically, weeds sticking out of dirt.

To make them feel welcome, he said.

On weekends he did gardening. Set up trellises against the tiny-house walls and planted flowers and vines to make it look picturesque.

His beer belly kept growing.

She decided he needed an incentive. To eat better again, at least.

"*I* know what you could do," she said one night after he brought home a large, greasy pizza and consumed the whole thing. Full of trans fats and loaded with pepperoni. Which was carcinogenic. "You could teach yourself Afghan cooking!"

She knew nothing about Afghan food. But she was fairly sure it wasn't pizza and fast-food burgers.

"That way, when they get here, you can have a supply laid in for them. So they don't have to knuckle down. And feel more at home. You know?"

"Interesting," he said, nodding.

He decided to test his first meal on Nick and Mia—invited them over for dinner.

"Mia, you know, is a vegetarian," Amy reminded him while he was toiling over the stove. The dishes involved lamb.

"Right, right," said Buzz. "Well, she can have the aushak."

"Aushak?"

"It's leek and scallion dumplings. And the boranee banjan. Mostly eggplant."

It struck her, watching him move around the kitchen, that she couldn't remember the last time he'd cooked for the family. She was the one who'd handled everyday food. Though he was a better cook.

She liked that Mia and Nick were an item. Mia'd been Liza's best friend since preschool. So it kept the families close. And Mia was such a sweet girl—volunteered at an assisted-living community.

But it made her nervous. What if they broke up? After a breakup came estrangement. Hard on *everyone*. His previous girlfriend had lasted for ten months, and they *never* saw her anymore.

That girlfriend had been more age-appropriate, by the calendar, but always seemed immature. She was always dressed up as a warrior priestess, or something. It was Halloween 365 days a year, for that girl.

So she tried to cultivate her own bond with Mia. That way, if she and Nick broke up, Mia would still see her as a friend. Or a confidante, at least.

"So, have you heard back?" she asked Mia when they came in. "On your college applications? I forgot to ask, last time we saw you."

"Yeah," said Mia, smiling. "I got into, like, three good ones."

"That's fantastic!"

"Vassar, Sarah Lawrence, and UCLA."

"Mia!" She hugged her. "I'm so proud of you."

"I was going to choose Vassar. But now I'm thinking UCLA. It's way cheaper. Plus I wouldn't have to move so far away."

"It's not *me* she'd miss," said Nick. He was carrying some folded boxes from Home Depot. Still moving his stuff out, in fits and starts. He propped up the boxes against the wall of the entryway. "She doesn't want to leave her friends at the old folks' home."

"Nick!" said Buzz, emerging from the kitchen with a dishtowel slung over his shoulder. He was wearing a KISS THE COOK apron.

To Buzz, whenever Nick came over it was like he'd been away for years. Though it was never longer than about three weeks.

They did a shoulder-to-shoulder hug, a man-clap on the back.

"So have you got your assignment yet?" asked Nick. "Are they coming?"

Buzz shook his head. "Any day now, though," he said. "We're getting close. I can feel it."

"You know," said Nick, "there are desperate migrants just two hours' drive from here who could use your help, too. If the people from halfway across the world aren't coming. Folks literally dying for some US hospitality. All along the border with Mexico."

"Well Nick, I can't exactly force the Border Patrol to hand over their Venezuelans," said Buzz. "Now can I."

"It's really great," said Mia. "What you're doing. I told the elders about it. A couple of *them* were refugees. This one lady's family escaped from Stalin. She was only six."

When they sat down and ate, it wasn't clear the kids were enjoying the food. Mia ate a single dumpling and a scoop of eggplant and said it was delicious—she just wasn't that hungry.

And Nick had always been a picky eater.

"Are you worried at all?" Mia asked when Buzz excused himself to go get the dessert.

"Worried about what?"

"Having new people living with you? From such a different culture? I think it's brave. But I might be anxious about it."

"You know," Amy confessed, "I *am* a little nervous."

"They'll be Muslims, correct?" said Nick.

"I assume," said Amy.

"They could be offended by our secular ways," said Nick.

"Your father's researched local mosques. And transit options. Because, I mean, we have two cars, but we're not sure how it would work. We could lend them my car . . . I don't know. It could be difficult for them. To take on LA traffic. Not being familiar with how people drive. Around here."

"You mean, like assholes?" said Nick.

"Well. Just in general."

"They gotta have asshole drivers there, too."

"We don't even know if one of them will have a driver's license. From there. They'll have to get a California one, anyway, but I mean, they could be from a rural place. And maybe they couldn't afford a car, back home."

"They could take Ubers," said Mia. "Couldn't they?"

"We'll have to get them a smartphone," nodded Amy. "If they don't have one."

After dessert, which was a dried-fruit confection Amy didn't care for, Mia suggested they take a stroll. Her house was about a ten-minute walk from theirs. They could drop in, she said. Her painter mother had a friend over, a prof at UCLA, and Mia figured she could say hi.

She didn't know if she'd ever take a class from her, she told Amy—she taught something obscure, like semiotics—but she could ask her questions in general.

"I'd love to see Helen," said Amy. "I haven't talked to her since Thanksgiving."

Buzz hemmed and hawed about joining them—he had to order a rug pad to go under the kilim, which kept sliding all over the place on the tiny house's slick, laminate floor—but finally agreed. After Nick nudged him and said, "Hey, Dad. This here is quality *family* time."

So they set out down the block. The sun was setting and the neighbors' gardens looked lush and green.

"Thanks to the Owens Valley," said Nick. "The lake that's now a bowl of dust."

"Old news," said Buzz.

"Have you ever been up there?" he asked them. They shook their heads. "There's a monument in the dry lakebed. With the shapes of the shorebirds cut into it. That used to live there before the Greater Los Angeles area took their water. You can look right through their empty silhouettes. At the cloudless sky."

He and Buzz fell behind, discussing aqueducts.

When they got to Mia's house, Amy followed her through the main rooms and out the sliders to a back patio. Where Helen and her friend sat on deck chairs. With a bottle of wine on a table.

The friend swiveled in her chair.

"*Trudy?*" said Amy. "What are *you* doing here?"

"Oh my God! Amy!" said Trudy.

"I didn't know you knew each other!" said Helen.

Trudy stood and they hugged.

"We were roommates in college!" said Amy. "How did *you* two meet?"

"I gave a talk to some art students at her school," said Helen. "About how to sell out successfully. As an artist."

"Oh, now," said Trudy. "It was about contemporary portraiture."

"Exactly."

"When Amy and I roomed together, she used to get all the guys," said Trudy. "Stiff competition."

"Oh, stop," said Amy.

"It's true. You were so blond and bouncy. Like a cheerleader."

"Well. When I bounce now, it's not a positive."

"We need more chairs," said Helen. "Mia. Could you bring out the ones we used for the ice cream social? From the garage?"

Then Nick and Buzz showed up. Helen went to get more wine, and they sat around talking. Trudy's teenage son was doing well, she reported. Some peer pressure issues, briefly. Mostly around pronouns. For a month or two he'd been a he/they, but then he got annoyed with it. Now he was back to he/him again.

And she was seeing someone.

Amy was surprised by that—she hadn't dated since her divorce, as far as Amy knew. Which had been, like, a decade ago.

"We're Mutt and Jeff," said Trudy. "He runs a food business and outweighs me maybe twofold."

"Who are Mutt and Jeff?" asked Mia.

Amy was glad Mia had asked. She didn't know either.

"It means a physically mismatched pair," explained Helen. "From an old comic strip."

"Nick," said Mia. "Are *we* like Mutt and Jeff?"

"Hell no," said Buzz. "You're more like bookends."

"Nick's so much taller, though."

"With Mel and me, it's a mental mismatch, too," said Trudy. "But somehow it works. So far, at least."

"Mel?" said Nick. "He doesn't own a fleet of food trucks, does he? Gourmet Mexican? And have a daughter named Chaya?"

Trudy stared at him.

"Talk about a small world," she said.

"Nick and Chaya used to be a couple!" said Mia.

"That's . . . Really? Wow," said Trudy.

"Mel's a good guy," said Nick. "Generous. I hope she's not still upset with me. Chaya."

"I don't think she ever mentioned you," said Trudy. "I would have registered it. You're the only Nick I know."

"Phew," said Nick.

"She has a new boyfriend. They dress up like vampires and go to role-playing events called World of Darkness. Or Blood and Fire."

"Vampires," said Nick. "Go figure."

As they were leaving, Trudy said to Helen and her, "I know. Let's do a hike together! Next weekend! Say, Runyon Canyon? Just the three of us?"

"I don't like to call them hikes," said Helen.

Her husband had died on a hike.

"Oh, I'm so sorry," said Trudy.

"How about a power walk?" suggested Amy.

"Sure," said Trudy. "A power walk, then."

"But without the power," said Helen. "After all, we're middle-aged white women."

She was glad to get out of the house. Buzz couldn't make his phone call rounds on weekends. Where he typically worked out some of his frustrations. So Saturdays and Sundays consisted of a lot of cooking of Afghan dishes, which were already filling up both freezers. He cooked and cooked, and meanwhile, on the kitchen counter, a propped-up iPad played videos of dusty brown camps and food lines.

Not even new. From when the news media was still bothering to cover them, Buzz said.

"Why do you watch those all the time?" she'd asked him this morning, grabbing an energy bar. "It seems masochistic."

"No, Amy, it's *reality*," he said.

When it came to the refugees, he had no sense of humor.

Heading up the trail, they passed a lot of dogs on leashes. And some loping along ahead of their owners with no leashes at all.

They'd run up, jump around, and sniff you. Making a beeline for the crotch.

Until their owners called them back.

"They're not supposed to be off-leash," said Trudy. "But I get it. People like their dogs to feel some freedom."

"Yeah, but their freedom shouldn't be sniffing my vagina," said Helen.

It was good to be away from Buzz's tireless industry. There was a lightness to it.

"I saw a coyote in my own yard," said Trudy. "The other day."

"*They* don't sniff crotches," said Helen. "Thank you, coyotes."

"I've seen them here too," said Amy. "A skinny one loping along the LA River. On the concrete."

"It gives you hope," said Trudy. "We tried to poison them into oblivion. And trap them. Still do. There's a government program that wipes out like sixty thousand every year. Across the whole country."

"Oh, no," said Amy. "Sixty *thousand*? But why?"

"Varmint control, supposedly. It's like those old Looney Tunes. On Saturday morning. Except we're the coyote, constantly trying out new methods of killing. And the real-life coyotes are the Road Runner."

"*Road* Runner," sang Helen, "the coyote's after you . . ."

"*Road* Runner," sang Amy, joining in. She still knew the tune. "If he catches you, you're through."

"They do it for the farmers and ranchers. But maybe also because they like to. It's their job description. They did the same thing with the wolves, way back when. And the wolves disappeared."

"They're trying to bring them back, though," said Helen. "I read about a couple of new packs. Up north of San Francisco."

At the summit they stopped and sat down on a bench.

"Last time I was here you could see smoke from a wildfire," said Helen. "It must have been back in September."

"Which fire was that?" asked Amy.

"I forget," said Helen.

They looked out over the city. Through the haze.

"This place was beautiful once," said Trudy. "Before we got here and ruined it."

"Who knows?" said Helen wistfully. "Maybe after we're gone, one day, it'll be beautiful again."

Amy had felt so buoyant, coming up. They'd all been buoyant. Now an odd melancholy had crept in.

What did Helen mean, after we're gone?

Them? Just the three of them?

They reminded her of Nick. Went from funny to dark in seconds.

Maybe they should go on antidepressants. Like him.

Was she the only one? Who wasn't a depressive?

On the way down she looked at the passing dogs and thought, What if Buzz had settled on a humbler project? Say, dog adoption?

It would have been so much easier. All you had to do was feed and walk them. And let them sniff some vaginas.

"I shouldn't say it, but part of me wishes Buzz had picked another obsession," she confided.

"You're not on board with the refugee-hosting?" asked Trudy.

"I am, in *theory*," she said.

"But not in practice?" said Helen.

"They just aren't *coming*," said Amy. "It's like, they're always about to, but then they never arrive. Once we got an assignment, but then they took it back again. So it's this major goal. That hovers endlessly."

"I feel that way in general," said Helen. "Like we're all waiting for something that never comes. A sign, maybe. Written across the sky by a thousand jet planes. In synchronicity. And once we see it, well, *then* we may do something. Meanwhile the smaller signs are all around. So many of them that together they *are* a giant sign. And we go on as if we don't see it."

"I've seen it," said Trudy. "I saw it a long time ago."

They walked.

Downhill, downhill, downhill.

"I recognize it," went on Trudy. "Like an old enemy whose name and face have faded over the years. But now and then, out of the corner of my eye, I get a glimpse. And I feel so cold. This terrible coldness down to the marrow of my bones."

"You do?" asked Amy, confused. "So, then . . . what is it, then?"

"Just the end."

"The end of what?"

Trudy didn't answer.

"Oh, honey," said Helen kindly. "Of everything."